AMERICAN Diaries

Summer MacCleary

VIRGINIA, 1749

⸻❈⸻

by Kathleen Duey

⸻❈⸻

Aladdin Paperbacks

For Richard
For Ever

First Aladdin Paperbacks edition July 1998

Copyright © 1998 by Kathleen Duey

Aladdin Paperbacks
An imprint of Simon & Schuster
Children's Publishing Division
1230 Avenue of the Americas
New York, NY 10020

Library of Congress Cataloging-in-Publication Data
Duey, Kathleen.
Summer MacCleary, Virginia, 1749 / Kathleen Duey.
— 1st Aladdin Paperbacks ed.
p.   cm. — (American diaries ; #10)
Summary: While working as an indentured servant on a plantation
in Virginia in 1749, thirteen-year-old Summer must prove her
innocence when her master's daughter accuses her of stealing.
ISBN 0-689-81623-5 (pbk)
[1. Indentured servants—Fiction. 2. Virginia—Social life and
customs—Colonial period, ca. 1600–1775—Fiction. 3. Slavery—
Fiction. 4. Stealing—Fiction.] I. Title. II. Series.
PZ7.D8694Su   1998
[Fic]—dc21   98-7218
CIP   AC

Quite late, using the end of my candle, little James sleeping sound. This day ends my sixth year at Weller Plantation and begins my seventh. I thought Letty might take note of the day. She used to, when we were little, but no more. Now she seems not to remember me as a friend at all. I suppose it is the way it must be.

I dreamed last night of Auntie Emily and my sisters and woke crying. I wrote to them this past Christmastide, then again in spring. Master Weller always gives my letters to ships' captains to deliver in London—but it is three years now since they have written me. I cannot help but worry. How I wish that Mother and Father had not died and that we could have all stayed together.

I did not have to help much with ironing today—Zilpha is quite over her fever—so I pretended to dust the parlor and listened in on Rob's tutor for a half hour or so. Today, Thomas Kyler talked at length about a book—The Spirit of the Laws, written by a Baron de Montesquieu (I have copied that spelling from the book spine itself and am sure of it!). It is in French so Rob cannot make it out yet. Thomas Kyler translated, reading aloud. The book says people's wealth or poverty, their religion and language—everything about them—affects what wars shall be fought and how laws are made. It all fits together, the book says, which only makes sense, if one thinks about it. I had many questions, and had to bite my tongue to hold them inside.

Thomas Kyler is teaching Rob about logic and reasoning now as well. I intend to try to use reason to solve any puzzles I find. Here is one solution I have come to this night: Fruit wood ashes make better lye than oak wood, and so, better soap.

Here is my reasoning: Soapmaking this past Friday, we used apple wood ashes from the smokehouse because the roasting of the pig on Thursday had fouled the kitchen hearth with spattered fat—and yesterday, on Wash Day, Zilpha said that the linens got clean easier and didn't need to be boiled for so long—a blessing for poor Fisk in this hot spell. So the lye must have been stronger. This could well be due to the fruit wood ashes—for the tallow was the same as we always use and bayberry was added only to the last batch, meant for bath soap.

My back is aching and my hands red and raw. I am always so content to be shut of soapmaking. It will take days before the stink of the tallow leaves the hearth. Letty was supposed to stir the tallow for me when I had to see to little James—then ran off to chase a lark she heard outside the door. I was only scolded, not willow-switched, bless Mistress Weller for her gentle heart. Letty, of course, barely noticed the scolding and didn't tell her mother she had agreed to watch the pot!

Letty is less my friend now than even a year ago. Dody is in the dairy; we almost never see her in the great house except to carry bathwater or help with some other heavy chore. How long ago were those pretend balls and parties we three played at so happily together!

James thrives this summer. He is strong for a five-months child and has two lower teeth now without too much illness. I will be relieved when he can use the standing stool for longer times without his little legs beginning to tremble. Myrna is wet-nursing him only four or five times a day now—not at all at night. Myrna doesn't swaddle her own little ones. Mistress Weller has tried to teach the slave women proper childrearing, but they refuse to learn. Myrna's older children all work the fields now.

Using arithmetic I have learned from Rob and his tutor, I calculated this today: On my twentieth birthday, James will be seven years, one month, and sixteen days old. It will be hard to leave him then, for all that I will be glad of my redemption papers and my indenture ending. He is a dear baby, with merry smiles. If he lives, he will be a cheerful boy and a good-humored man.

The great house is more peaceful this summer: Collier is gone off to London for his education. Rob is fourteen now, just a year past my own age. He is kind, if arrogant, and not mean-hearted as Collier was to the slaves and servants. Anna is acting the part of mistress lately—her face stern and somber much of the time. Letty is in an odd humor as well. She was angry with me for no reason on bath day when I came in with her clean drawers. She nearly knocked the flannels into the basin.

I will soon be out of fresh paper to write. I wish I

could ask Letty for her sketchbook. It is just like this one, but empty, as she refuses to draw—as we were both supposed to. My first ten pages are poems and essays on what I hear at Rob's lessons. The next five are reserved for new arithmetic as (and if!) I manage to learn—but after that, I have written this diary of my days. I ought to destroy it, but I find myself putting it back beneath my ticking instead. It is precious to me.

I will put away my quill because I hear someone in the passage. Perhaps Rob and Thomas Kyler are prowling toward the cookhouse for a midnight meal? I will snuff my candle so they will not see the light beneath the door.

What is this? I think I hear someone weeping. . . .

CHAPTER ONE

Summer waved her diary back and forth to dry the ink, wrinkling her nose at the acrid smoke that rose from her snuffed candle. The footsteps in the passage came closer and so did the sound of sniffling. Summer tensed at the light scratching on her door. Whatever was the matter, her aching back and lye-scalded skin and sleep-heavy eyelids wanted no part of it.

"Summer!" the whisper was insistent.

Summer made a small sound, like someone who was turning over in sleep, then fell silent again, as she closed her diary and skidded it beneath her cot. She pulled her nightcap on, knowing who it was, knowing she would have to open the door.

"Summer?"

This time the whisper was softer, piteous. Summer gave in and sat up on her cot.

"Who is there?"

"It's Letty!"

Summer sighed. Poor Letty sounded miserable. It had been so long since she had turned to Summer for friendship. Something had to be terribly wrong to bring her here in the middle of the night. Summer stood up and crossed the smooth plank floor to the door, feeling her way along the wall until she could find the leather door strap in the dark. She pulled it and the door opened.

Letty slipped inside, already whispering. "Oh, Summer, you have to help me. You must!"

"Whatever is the matter?" Summer reached out in the darkness to touch Letty's cheek. It was wet with tears. Awful thoughts came into Summer's mind. "Is everyone, is your mother or—"

"Everyone is all right," Letty cut her off, sounding irritated at the interruption. "Everyone but me." She began to sniffle and cry again. Summer could not see her, could not even make out her shape.

"Where is your candle, Letty?"

"In my room. I put it out hours ago," Letty said softly. "But I cannot sleep. Will you light yours for me?"

"Wait." Summer felt her way back to her cot and found her own candle stub in its little pewter holder on the floor. "I'll have to go out to the cookhouse," she said, straightening, hoping Letty would tell her not to bother. But Letty just sniffled a little louder. Summer heard her crossing the room, then felt the brush of

Letty's night shift as she sank onto the edge of the cot.

"Please do hurry," Letty sighed, and Summer could imagine the exaggerated, sorrowful expression on her face.

"Be quiet enough not to waken your little brother," Summer whispered, gesturing toward James's cradle, even though in the darkness, Letty had no chance of seeing her. "If James begins to cry and I am not here to quiet him, it'll bring your mother down the passageway."

Letty did not answer.

"Promise you will not awaken him," Summer insisted, whispering.

Letty made some reply in a hiccuping voice and went back to her crying.

Summer slipped out the door and started down the passageway. She tiptoed past Letty's and Anna's bedchamber, then the larger room where Rob slept. Then, she began to move quietly past the grandest bedchamber. Her master and mistress were slumbering there in the heavy four-poster bed with its gauzy curtains to keep mosquitoes out. She imagined the luxury of their feather-stuffed ticking and yawned, wishing Letty had waited until morning. Then she felt guilty for being unkind. But Letty had been so difficult lately!

Near the end of the passage, Summer thought she heard a sound and paused to look back, staring into the darkness. What if Letty noticed the foul odor of the wet ink? Would she poke around beneath the cot? And if she touched the cover of the sketchbook, she would know, even without a candle, what it was. Letty was curious to a fault, in any circumstance. But knowing her father's view on the education of girls, she would be especially nosy as to what Summer might be writing so secretively. Summer was glad Letty had no candle with her.

Moving silently toward the door, trailing the fingers of her right hand along the wall to guide herself, Summer resolved to hide her diary better from now on, just in case. If Master Weller ever read her philosophical thoughts, saw all the wild imaginings spurred by overhearing Thomas Kyler's tutorial sessions with Rob—he would be livid. And the arithmetic! Numbers and ciphering beyond keeping household accounts was hardly a proper feminine pursuit.

Master Weller would certainly take the book. He wouldn't want her around his own daughters—perhaps wouldn't want her to stay in the great house at all. It would be awful. Summer shook her head, angry with herself. This was hardly the first time that she had had these thoughts, and still she kept the book.

"I will destroy it tomorrow," she promised herself. "I will burn it in the cooking hearth while Paris is out at the cabins."

Summer's searching fingers finally found the

door in the dark. She could still hear Letty, sniffling away and making a piteous, tiny whimpering like a frightened kitten in the silence of the night.

Her bare feet quiet on the clean planked floor, Summer unbarred the door, careful to make no sound—this door was almost straight opposite her master's bedchamber. She slipped outside and glanced up at the starry sky. It scared her to be out alone at night, and she was risking a sharp scolding for opening the house door at all. She shuddered, looking around, unable to see any of the outbuildings clearly. It was so dark.

Too bad it was July and so warm out, Summer thought as she hurried along the wooden walkway. If it had been colder, there'd have been a parlor fire and no need to go out to the cookhouse. Summer pulled the latchstring, then pushed open the heavy door and went inside. In just a moment or two, she told herself, she would get her candle lit. The little globe of gold-ish light would push back the night and keep it away from her.

The hearth was full of white ashes, heaped highest in three places where Paris's supper fires had been. Summer knelt beside the stew fire and blew lightly, clearing a patch of hot orange coals.

Working in the dim light, she picked one of Paris's long rice straws from its cow's horn holder and touched it to the embers. When it began to give off a spiraling plume of sickly sweet smoke, she breathed on it again and it burst into flame.

Summer lit the candle and stood up, leveling the little pewter holder in her right hand. With her left, she shielded the flame from the air stirred by her movement. The kitchen still smelled strongly of the lye from soapmaking—with the odors of roast meat and boiled corn on top of it. Summer wrinkled her nose as she went out the door, closing it behind herself.

Careful to protect the candle flame, Summer hurried along the walkway as fast as she dared, then lowered the candle as she neared the door. Instinctively turning her back to the sigh of a breeze that made the candle flicker, she pressed on the door to reenter the house.

Instead of swinging easily inward, the door stood fast. Startled, Summer pushed harder, then stepped back, disbelieving. The door wouldn't budge. She set down her candle, uneasily aware of the endless black night that began just behind her and stretched out all the way to the Chesapeake, to the ocean, all the way home to London. Resettling her nightcap, Summer put her shoulder against the door and shoved hard. Still, it would not move.

Her heart beating wildly, her mind supplying images of thieves and strollers and dangerous snakes, she stood still, trying to understand. It was impossible, but what else could have happened? Someone had barred the door from the inside. Summer tried to imagine who would have locked her out. And, most puzzling of all, *why?*

CHAPTER TWO

Summer fought an urge to beat on the door with her fists. She heard the whine of a mosquito and slapped at it, careful not to disturb the candle flame. She glanced over her shoulder at the dark home yard. She couldn't see even as far as the springhouse, much less beyond it to the garden. Where was Letty? Had she just wandered back to her own bed? Why would she have bolted the door?

Summer pushed on the door again, willing it to give, trying to believe this was all a mistake. But it did not budge, and a tiny rill of breeze fluttered at the candle flame. Summer cupped her left hand closer around it.

If the candle went out, she could just go back to the hearth and light it once more. But it was only a stub, one of the little candle pieces Mistress Weller tossed into the copper bin to be remelted and strained and added to the next batch of tallow wax. It wasn't going to last long.

Summer took a slow breath. She would soon be standing in the dark, alone, locked out of the house. And James would cry before long. He always did, just after midnight, and she patted him until he slept soundly again.

Summer thought about taking a candle—a new, whole one—from the box that lay on the cool larder floor. But as much as the dark scared her, she knew she wouldn't dare. Mistress Weller kept accounts of everything in her household. She would miss a candle and demand that the difference be accounted for. *And how would I ever explain this?* Summer thought.

She tried scratching lightly at the door. There was no response from within. She stood very still, listening, for as long as she could stand it. Then she scratched at the wood once more. There was still no sound at all from inside the house.

"Think!" Summer commanded herself, squeezing her eyes shut, hard, to quell the tears she could feel rising. The parlor door and the storeroom door at the other end of the house would be barred now, of course. There were two sash windows in the parlor, but they were latched fast every night before bed as well. There was simply no way to get into the house unless someone let her in.

Summer tried to sweep her stray thoughts together, to examine them logically, as Thomas Kyler always admonished Rob to do. Letty had been upset over something. But what? And no matter how upset she was, she would not bar the door against Summer, would she? Letty was often thoughtless, especially when she was peevish or bored. But still . . .

Perhaps Anna had awakened and barred the door, not knowing anyone was outside. But Letty knew and would tell her older sister, wouldn't she? Summer sighed. If it were not for James, she could have curled up beside the cookhouse hearth and waited for morning. Paris would see her when she came in to build up the fires for breakfast, and maybe Dody, if she came up from the slave quarters with Paris, but neither of them would say a word to Mistress Weller if Summer asked them not to.

"But James will cry between now and morning," Summer whispered to herself. "He always does."

Summer bit at her lip, rubbing at the door again, patting it lightly with her palm. She was afraid to make very much noise. She didn't want to bring Master Weller from his bed—or Mistress Weller. Or, if Anna had been the one to bar the door then return to bed, Summer loathed to wake her again. Anna was so stern now. It would not be long before she married, a few years at most, Summer thought. Mistress Weller was constantly telling her older daughter how a household should be run.

Summer shivered, even though she wasn't cold, and tried the door again. It still wouldn't budge. She rested her forehead on the wood, then straightened, glancing down at her candle. Not too much longer, and she would be in the dark. What if Anna had made Letty go back to bed?

Summer thought about her sketchbook, with all its writing and arithmetical problems, just lying on the floor beneath her cot, easy to see once daylight came. Easy to find. Master Weller often referred to a book he had had Captain Chrislen bring from England—*The Education of a Daughter*. He used it to guide his raising of Letty and Anna. Summer had seen him hunched over his candle, reading it on nights when Anna or Letty had been at some mischief during the day.

Summer had managed to read parts of it, secretly, when she was supposed to be cleaning the floor of Master Weller's study, sweeping up tobacco and food crumbs and dusting his books. The author, Archbishop Fenelon, discussed in detail how too much learning could upset the feminine mind. Summer wondered if that was as true as the archbishop seemed to think. After all, he had written the book in 1687—sixty-two years ago! Perhaps women's minds had changed in that time. Or perhaps it had never been true.

Summer never felt upset or uneasy after she listened to Thomas Kyler instruct Collier and Rob. Much of what they discussed was more interesting than the dogtrot of each day's house chores. She was already learning most of what anyone ever needed to know about *that*.

"Letty?" Summer pleaded with the closed door. How much time had gone past? It felt like half the night, even though she knew it could not have been more than a few minutes. "Letty, *please!*"

There was no stirring from within. Summer pressed her ear against the wood. Was James crying yet? She wasn't sure she would be able to hear him from outside. "Letty, *please?*" Summer whispered, wishing she dared to shout. "Please, *anyone!*"

As if her words had finally been desperate enough to influence Letty, Summer heard the bar sliding to the side. A second later the door opened and she stepped back, hoping it was Letty, not Anna. As candlelight spilled out into the night, Summer caught her breath. It wasn't either one of the sisters. It was Master Weller.

"Summer! What are you doing outdoors? What is the matter?" he demanded. He was trying to whisper and it turned his usually deep voice into a rasp.

"I came out to the cookhouse to relight my candle," Summer managed, her heart knocking at her ribs, unsure just what to say. She glanced up at him, lifting her candle just enough to try to read his face before she said more. Why was he prowling about the house this time of night? Had Letty awakened him with her sniffling? Or was James crying?

Master Weller held a long, new candle, lit from the narrow hearth in his bedchamber, she was sure. He had not planned to rise at midnight like this or he'd have saved a bit of a stub to light. Zilpha would have laid out this new one for the following evening.

Master Weller's nightcap was askew, and Summer could see his brown and gray hair stubble and the rubbed places on his temples from his wig. He was frowning. "Why? What need do you have of light in the middle of the night?"

Summer opened her mouth, then closed it. If she told him Letty had awakened her upset and crying, he would question Letty. If whatever had caused Letty to cry was something she was hiding from her father, she would get angry at Summer for tattling secrets. Summer glanced up to see Master Weller staring at her, his face wrinkled into a frown. Just then, she heard a thin wail come down the passage.

"James!" she breathed.

Master Weller stepped aside, but he gripped her shoulder when she tried to go in. "Summer. I won't have you cat-footing around at night like this. You are to stay within the house."

"Yes, Master Weller." Summer looked up into his eyes, remembering two years before when Collier had come home after dark more than half the time, it had seemed like—often smelling of hard cider or rum, always flushed and excited from crowded cock fights or horse races or boxing matches. No one had ever said a word to him.

Suddenly, just at the edge of the amber light cast by Master Weller's candle, Summer saw a flash of movement in the dark passage. An instant later, Letty was poking her head out the door, startling her father so that he stepped away from her.

"Letty! Now what are you doing out of your bed?"

Letty smiled sweetly. "I heard you moving about, Father. I wanted to make sure that nothing was wrong." She looked out the door and smiled again. "Summer? Whatever are you doing up?"

Summer stared at Letty, taken so by surprise that she could not answer.

"Why is she out there, Father?" Letty asked, looking up at him. Summer could hear James whimpering down the passage. He was crying a little louder now. Letty heard, too, and arched her brows. "Poor little James, left alone to cry."

"Go back to your bedchamber, Letty," Master Weller said in a sharp tone, then he remembered the need for quiet and lowered his voice again. "If Anna wakens and misses you, she'll set the whole house astir."

Letty made her father a little curtsy and padded off down the passage. Summer blinked, still trying to think what to say. Now, if she told Master Weller that

Letty had come to her room, crying, he would likely think she was making it up, her imagination prompted by Letty's appearance.

Summer watched him glance fondly at Letty as she walked away. There was no point in explaining what had really happened. If he believed her at all, he would only scold Letty. And that would only make her angry. Whatever she was up to, pretending to be surprised like this, it would only get worse.

"Did you come out your little window?" Master Weller turned back to stare at Summer, waiting.

"Of course not," Summer said automatically, then hesitated. "Perhaps as I came out, I caught the end of the bar on my sleeve and pulled it—" she began, but he interrupted her.

"The bar was entirely in place, Summer. I don't pretend to know what has happened here, but it could not simply slide itself in. Did you sneak out a window and then have trouble climbing back inside? Do you understand the danger outside at night?"

"Yes," Summer said contritely, knowing it was useless to try to explain. "I am sorry, Master Weller." She shivered and he drew her inside, then slid the lock bar back into place. When he turned, Summer lowered her candle and held it out to one side so that he could not see into her eyes as easily. Her unhappy, confused thoughts would surely show. Poor little James cried louder.

"Go walk the little one about before his crying wakens everyone," Master Weller said abruptly.

Summer nodded gratefully. "Yes, Master Weller. I will do that." She came forward as he stepped out of her way, releasing her from his scrutiny.

"I will want to speak with you again about this when I return from Court Day," he said as she passed him.

"Yes, Master Weller," she said meekly, and kept walking. If she was fortunate, he might forget. The plantation required his attention daily—often there were problems that caused him to saddle his tall black gelding and ride off with Mr. Eagan, the overseer, their coattails flying and their faces intent.

Or maybe, if Court Day was exciting with case after case that either made him angry or involved him personally in some land dispute or the poll-tax argument or some other concern—a matter so small as the indentured girl's wandering about at night would escape his mind altogether. Summer turned into her chamber and set the pewter candleholder down on the sea chest that served as her bed table. The wick was smoking badly and she trimmed it with her fingers, brushing them quickly against her nightgown. The noxious smell of burned tallow rose, then abated.

"There now," Summer crooned, crossing to the cradle. "There now, I am here, little one." She picked James up, marveling at how heavy he was getting. He quieted the instant she had him in her arms. She could feel how wet he was and decided to change his swaddling now. Why not? She was hardly ready to sleep, thanks to Letty, and it would save her the chore first thing in the morning.

Summer gauged the candle stub. There was a little more than an inch of it left and the wick looked straight and strong. If she hurried, she would have time before it guttered and went out.

The soft swaddling cloths were hung from hooks set high on the wall especially for the purpose. Beside them was a bench with a thick flannel laid across it. The four extra straight pins pierced the flannel's edge—never to be used unless one of the usual six was hopelessly lost. Mistress Weller was very strict about pins.

Summer laid out a fresh clout rag, and a cloth and water basin. Everything a baby needed was close to hand. This room had been the cradle room of all the Weller children except Collier. When Collier had been little, Master and Mistress Weller had lived in the house Sam Eagan, the overseer, lived in now.

Summer opened the drawer that held the little ribbon-tie shirts for James—actually they had been Rob's, and Collier's before him. The next drawer down held Collier's long petticoats, which had already been passed down to Rob, then Anna, then Letty. James would need them in another month or two, when

Mistress Weller decided his arms and legs were well enough formed to risk unswaddling him.

"Lie still," Summer said to James. He wrinkled up his brow and stared at her intently. His hair was finally getting thick enough to cover his skull. It made him look like a little man.

Summer smiled at him and began unwrapping the long strip of linen that bound his legs together. Working fast from long practice, she undid the bandaging that held his arms straight. Last, she undid the shoulder pins that anchored the stay band around James's forehead.

She cleaned his bottom with a wet rag, then rubbed a little rosemary and lard from the tin Paris had given her onto his skin. It was helping. The red welts were getting better. Once he was out of his swaddling cloth, the rashes would disappear, Paris said.

"Dear little James," Summer singsonged. His cheeks were puffed out as he made his new sound— an odd little huffing noise that Rob had taught him. Then he kicked his legs wildly and beat his arms up and down as she reached up for clean swaddling cloths.

By the time Summer had James's legs rewrapped, the extra wad of linen positioned between his ankles as Mistress Weller had instructed her, his knees straight and aligned perfectly, the candle was about to go out. She settled him into his cradle, glad that his skull had closed completely and that she was through with the chore of pressing at his scalp every time she changed him. She pulled his blankets high around his neck and kissed his cheek. He tried to turn his head to look at her, but the stay band kept it straight.

As the candle began to flicker wildly, casting strange shadows on the walls, Summer lingered, patting James lightly, soothing him. He finally closed his eyes and half a minute later the candle guttered, releasing a puff of smelly smoke as it died.

Summer patted James a little longer, yawning. Finally, she tiptoed to her bed and sat on the edge, the rice straw crackling beneath her weight.

"Whatever is Letty up to?" she whispered into the darkness. She lay down and stared upward at the blackness. Then she remembered her diary, thrust hastily beneath her bed. She turned to her stomach and leaned down, reaching for it.

After a moment, Summer slid out of bed and knelt on the floor, searching the floor with her fingertips, unable to see anything at all. At first, she stilled her heart by telling herself that she had pushed her sketchbook farther under than she'd thought, but as the seconds ticked past and her searching hands found nothing, she felt a cold lump of worry forming in her belly. It was gone. Her diary was gone!

CHAPTER THREE

Baking Day dawned clear and promised fair. Summer opened her eyes to the little sounds that James always made upon waking. He was a quiet, dear baby. She hummed a little and heard his cooing sounds change—he knew she was awake.

Summer blinked and stretched. Then, abruptly, she remembered the nonsensical goings-on of the night before. She rolled out of bed and looked beneath her cot, hoping that somehow her diary had eluded her fingers and was still there. It wasn't.

"Morning, Missy Summer," Paris's voice came through the door. "Myrna came up to help me with carrying flour barrels and thought she would just take James with her now."

"I'm coming, Paris," Summer called out. Then she straightened her chemise and hurried to the cradle. She lifted James out and kissed his rosy cheek as he blinked and yawned. He wiggled against the swaddling as she carried his stiff little form to the door and opened it.

"Good morning," Myrna said softly to James. She and Paris didn't look much alike, but anyone could have told they were sisters from their voices. Summer smiled as James began his babbling at Myrna.

"You come on then," Myrna said in a low, cajoling tone. "Let's go get you fed some breakfast." She lifted James high, then settled him against her side as she reached out to touch Summer's cheek with her free hand. "You look sad. Is something wrong?"

Summer shook her head quickly. Myrna was the one all the slaves asked to conjure for them, or to heal them if they got sick or hurt. Her dark eyes were fixed on Summer's and it felt like she was looking right into her heart. Paris said that Myrna had always been that way, looking through folks, ever since she was a little girl. Master Weller said her conjuring was nonsense and sinful. But a lot of folks went to Myrna just the same.

"You tell me if something is worrying you," Myrna said gently. "I can help, maybe. Make you a charm or something."

"You know Marse Weller doesn't want you to talk like that," Paris interrupted, whispering.

Myrna smiled. "Summer won't tattle."

Summer shook her head. "Of course not." For a second, she thought about telling Myrna and Paris about everything that had happened in the night. Then she bit her lip. If she did, they would whisper to the other slaves and then Dody might say something to Letty.

Dody and Letty were almost exactly the same age, and even though Mistress Weller didn't want Dody in the great house anymore, she and Letty still talked sometimes, Summer was pretty sure. Summer missed Dody's sunny smiles and sweet nature.

"Rob! Time to rise!" The masculine shout came down the passageway. Summer recognized Thomas Kyler's voice. He usually sprang early from his bed in the storage room loft.

Paris rolled her eyes and shook her head as she looked up the passageway. "There he stands, like a rooster calling the sun. Baking Day has begun now, I suppose."

Summer laughed with Paris and Myrna as they turned to leave. She pulled her door shut, then whirled around the little room, straightening everything, shaking out the swaddling that was drying on the hooks. Fisk would come gather it up. Poor Fisk. He hated laundrying, she knew, bitterly resented having to do women's work. But since his foot had been mangled in the flax brake, he was no good for field work. Sometimes he helped old Ephrim with his joinery and repairs on the cabins—but most of his time was spent in the washhouse.

Summer lay her nightcap at the top of her cot and yanked her comb through her hair. Then she tucked up her bed linens, smoothing them with both hands—Mistress Weller hated a messy bedstead. Then she turned to the clothes hooks beside the door.

"Rob?" Thomas Kyler's voice came again. He was closer now, probably just outside Rob's door. "I am going with your father to Court Day. He says you are to stay to host guests who are coming later. He says you must finish with me first."

A protesting shout from the boys' chamber made Summer smile wryly. Rob would hate missing Court Day. Summer liked Rob well enough—especially now that Collier was gone. Collier had changed the day his father had given him a fine horse and a slave. From that day onward, Collier had begun to ride the tobacco fields, daring anyone to interfere with him, Toby riding behind on an old mare, trying to keep up. Summer had heard Mistress Weller lament the change in Collier many times and Summer knew she feared it coming in Rob as well. But maybe it wouldn't. Rob was kinder.

Summer dressed slowly. Her stays felt strange and stiff over her chemise this morning. She laced the corset tightly, knowing that Mistress Weller would be particularly critical of her appearance if company was coming. She stepped into her petticoat and tied the string around her waist. Then she slid her dress over her head.

The hem hung unevenly and Summer tugged

impatiently at the bodice, angry with herself over her sketchbook. She had been foolish to write improper thoughts and arithmetic lessons in it—even more foolish to have kept it all this time. If Letty did show her parents, Master Weller was going to be furious. And there was no telling what Letty might do—or why. Nothing that had happened the night before made any sense at all.

"Master Weller wouldn't sell my contract, though," Summer murmured to herself. "He would just warn me away from listening to Thomas Kyler when he is teaching Rob."

Summer tried to believe it. But the truth was, Master Weller had talked about selling her contract before when he was upset with her for one reason or another. Letty had told her about it. They had two or three likely slave girls about the right age to learn housework—and slaves were cheaper than indentureds.

Summer understood why. Paris had explained it. The slave girls would grow up learning how to work in the house or the fields and the time it took to teach them would be paid back over the years. And most of them would someday have children—those children would be Master Weller's slaves as well. Indentureds went free once their contracts were up—all that training and teaching walked right out the front door. Summer had heard Thomas Kyler tell

Rob one day that with more slaves in Virginia all the time, soon only charitable fools would buy indenture contracts.

Shivering even though it was not cold, Summer fussed with her dress, reaching up underneath to arrange her chemise, grateful that she wasn't expected to wear hoops. She finally managed to pull her hemline straight. Then she smoothed her dress and pinned on her apron, her hands a little trembly.

"I have to get the sketchbook back," Summer told herself sternly. "Somehow, I must get it back and throw it in the hearth and burn it up."

"Children?" Mistress Weller's sharp voice came from the passageway. "Letty? Anna? Rob, you, too!"

Summer stiffened at the tight, angry tone—usually Mistress Weller spoke very gently when she was correcting the servants or slaves, even when she was quite upset. Something had to be terribly wrong for her to speak to her children like this.

Summer opened her door an inch and peeked out. Mistress Weller was standing in the passage. Even this early, she was fully dressed, her hoops wide enough to be fashionable, her petticoats showing an embroidered edge from beneath her deep blue overskirt. Her wig was straight and well powdered. Summer could see a dusting of chalk on her lace-edged bodice.

"I want to speak to everyone," Mistress Weller

went on. "You, as well, Mr. Kyler. . . ." Summer fought an urge to close the door when Mistress Weller's eyes fell upon hers.

"Summer, if you are dressed, stop peeking and come join us," Mistress Weller said curtly.

Summer pushed the door open and came out. She stood politely, nervous, avoiding everyone's eyes. She swallowed and her throat felt tight.

"I apologize, Mother," Rob said as he came into the passageway. "I overslept a bit, I suppose. I—"

"Where is Toby?" Mistress Weller asked him.

Rob shrugged. "Maybe still asleep."

His mother clicked her tongue. "Collier kept him sharp. You are spoiling him into laziness."

Rob shrugged again. "I never need him this early for anything—he brings in the basin of wash water before bed at night and the chamber pot can wait. He serves me very well, Mother."

"Mistress?" It was Paris's low, musical voice. "You asked to see the baby?"

Summer turned to see her hurrying up the passage carrying James. He was content now, his belly full and his eyes heavy with sleepiness. Summer took him from Paris, holding him out when Mistress Weller reached for him. She smiled and all her cold curtness dissolved as she kissed her youngest son. Through the linen wrappings, she pinched at him gently, feeling his legs one at a time, then his arms.

"In a week or two I think we can free his arms, Summer," she said, her voice warmer. Then it cooled again. "Put him in his cradle and come back, please."

Summer felt breathless and lightheaded as she tucked James under his light cotton blanket. What was going on? Was it anything to do with her sketchbook? As she went back into the passage, she saw that Letty and Anna had joined the group, as well as Zilpha, the older slave woman who was housekeeper and served as the girls' chambermaid as well.

"I have something to tell all of you," Mistress Weller began when they had all quieted down. "And I wanted my children to be here when I say it. I want them to watch your faces with me, to see if any of us can discern guilt in your expressions."

Summer held her breath.

"My grandmother's ring is missing," Mistress Weller said quietly. "It means a great deal to me."

"Oh, Mother!" Letty cried out. She took Mistress Weller's hand and held it close to her cheek.

Anna sighed and looked sad. "Are you sure, Mother? Could you have mislaid it?"

Mistress Weller shook her head. "I do not wear it often, but I keep it in a very safe place. Someone looked very thoroughly in my chamber to have found it." Her eyes were narrowed. "I shall catch the thief, have no fear. I will not allow a thief to live in this house!"

Summer glanced around. The slaves' faces were bleak, but composed. Paris made a clicking sound with her tongue. Zilpha and Fisk looked stricken. Toby was looking at the floor with steady, patient eyes. Anna and Rob were glancing from one face to the next. Summer was afraid to look at any of them—especially Letty.

"I expect to have the ring returned," Mistress Weller was saying. "I expect you to return it to my chamber, if you are too cowardly to simply place it in my hand."

No one spoke. No one moved. Summer shot a quick glance at Letty. Her face was pale except for two round patches of color like a fever flush on her cheeks. She met Summer's eyes and a crooked smiled shaped her lips.

Mistress Weller was clearing her throat, her eyes flooded with tears. "Go on about your work, then, all of you. Nothing will stop me from finding the thief. If you know anything, any of you, if you noticed anything out of the ordinary, I expect you to tell me."

Letty waited until her mother had gone and the others were all turning away. Then she leaned close to Summer. "Who do you suppose took it? Did you?" she whispered, her breath tickling Summer's ear.

Summer stared at her. "Of course not. Where's my sketchbook?"

Letty waggled a finger at her. "What were you

doing outside last night? Hiding my mother's ring? Where did you put it? In your ear? On the moon? Beneath the tenth plank on the cookhouse walk?"

Summer stood rooted to the floor by the anger in Letty's voice as she spun around, sending her hooped skirt into a cascade of silken jounces as she walked away.

CHAPTER FOUR

Anna and Rob were in the parlor talking in low voices when Summer walked past on her way out to the cookhouse. They both glanced up and she ducked her head respectfully, then lifted it again, terrified that lowering her eyes would make them think her guilty.

"Where is James?" Anna called through the open door.

"Sleeping," Summer called back. "I am to help Paris today while he sleeps." Anna nodded brusquely, an expression of exaggerated seriousness on her face.

Once outside, with the heavy door shut safely behind her, Summer could not resist stopping on the house porch to stare at the planked path beneath her feet. There were no windows on this side of the house except the parlor window—and the draperies were always drawn across it to keep the sun off Mistress Weller's carpet.

Summer counted the planks, skipping her eyes from one to the next—eight, nine . . . ten. The tenth plank seemed to be a little wider than the ones on either side of it. But it was pegged down tightly to the broad, parallel timbers that supported the walkway. Summer glanced around again. Beneath it? What could Letty have possibly meant by *beneath* it? Or had she just been making up nonsense to be mean?

Summer tried to remember if there had been anything in her diary that would have made Letty think her guilty of stealing the ring. Almost without meaning to, she walked forward slowly, one small step at a time, half turning, watching the door of the springhouse, glancing up the path that led to the well, then the slaves' necessary out past the garden.

There were almost certainly slaves awake and going about their work. Fisk might already be in the washhouse, building a fire underneath the huge laundry cauldron. Dody was in the dairy still, no doubt, just getting started on her day's work, with Frieda snapping at her about every little piece of straw or cow hair in the milk.

Frieda was indentured, too, but for longer than Summer was. Her redemption papers wouldn't be drawn up until she was thirty-nine, if she lived that long. Would Mistress Weller talk to Frieda and Ephrim and the others about her ring?

Summer tried to remember what work old Ephrim would be at this morning. He was often about the great house, fixing this or that. He could still be reshingling the roofs of the slave cabins. Fisk might be out there helping him as well. Monday had been fair and fine and most of the wash had gotten done on time. Summer listened and caught the faint pinging of a hammer from the other side of the great house. Ephrim was splitting shakes, striking the wedge with his hammer.

Summer realized she was still stopped on the tenth plank and glanced around to see if anyone had seen her standing, thinking, staring at the sun-grayed oak wood. Letty was the one person who knew exactly why she had been outside last night. Why would she taunt her with foolishness about where the ring was hidden? In her ear, on the moon. . . .

Summer looked around once more, then, following her impulse, dropped to the ground and bent low to peer beneath the walk. In that instant she heard the creak of the cookhouse door.

"Whatever are you doing, child?"

Summer scrambled back to her feet, blushing, shaking the sand from her skirt. "Nothing."

Paris shook her head and put her hands on her hips. "Mistress wants you to help me put up pickles this morning while Marse James finishes his sleeping."

Summer nodded.

"I mean to begin one batch of sweets and one of sours this morning," Paris was saying slowly and distinctly, smiling at Summer patiently. "I've saved up some good thick rinds from the garden, and there's a half peck of those little tiny squash for dilling that Mistress likes so much the way I do them."

Summer nodded, but the words were not sticking in her mind. After a few seconds, she realized that Paris was staring at her. "It will all pass over, child," she said soothingly. "You ain't done nothing, have you?"

Summer shook her head.

"Then don't you worry. Whoever has done it will likely get caught. But if not, it's not your worry nor mine. Innocence proclaims itself, child."

Summer hugged Paris quickly, then backed away, wishing she could tell Paris about the things she had written in her sketchbook.

"If you fetch the honey jug, I'll get the vinegar and the dill out of the storeroom," Paris was saying. "I want to make sure that last kettle's worth of soap hardened up as well—the one Letty left off stirring."

Summer nodded. She watched Paris step off the boardwalk and head for the slant-roofed shed that stood just behind the cookhouse. The bottled goods were there, the soap molds and candle strings—anything that the mice wouldn't chew their way into. The root cellar was out there, too, steps leading down from the storeroom floor.

Summer went through the cookhouse door and headed for the pantry that was built along the back wall. The honey jug was heavy, and it sat on a low shelf. As she hoisted it upward, the bottom dripped water from the little trough it had been set in to keep the ants out.

"Paris?"

It was Toby's voice from the cookhouse door. There was something in his tone that made Summer hesitate. She stood still, listening as he came in.

"Paris, are you here?"

Without meaning to, Summer turned a little, accidentally clicking the honey jug against the china canister that held Mistress Weller's favorite tea.

"Paris, listen to me," Toby said in a lowered voice. "I saw Missy Anna tippy-toeing out behind the quarters an hour before sunrise. That girl was down on her knees in her pretty dress, scratching around in the dirt. If she has her mama's ring, it'll get terrible for all of us in the great house until they find a thief they can whip. Ain't nobody going to believe it was her, that's certain."

Toby was silent a moment and Summer heard Master Weller's voice, calling in the distance—probably from the stables. "He wants his saddle oiled and Garth is busy with the foaling mare," Toby said, then Summer heard him step back and close the door.

Summer exhaled slowly, trying to make sense out of what Toby had said. "Would *Anna* have stolen the ring?" Summer breathed. She backed out of the pantry and set the honey jug on the heavy worktable, staring at the worn oak surface. It had been scarred by twenty years' worth of knives.

"I just saw Toby," Paris said, opening the cookhouse door and scattering Summer's thoughts. "That man is so wrought up with all this that he wasn't making sense at all. Asked me how I'd gotten out of the kitchen."

"He came here looking for you," Summer said quickly. "I was in the pantry and he just started talking and—"

"You just listened."

Summer blushed, then nodded. Paris's face softened. "I didn't even let him get started. I told him what I told you. If you aren't the one, don't worry about it."

"But do you think Anna—"

"Toby is right about one thing," Paris said heavily, interrupting her. "If it was one of the Marse's family, we are all in for more trouble than we need. They will never believe it's one of the girls and they will punish whoever tries to say so."

Summer kept still, imagining it. Both Master Weller and Mistress Weller disliked scolding their children. That was half the reason they had secured Thomas Kyler, she knew. Mr. Otis Jenkins, the first tutor, had been too old to chase Collier over the countryside. Thomas Kyler was young enough to be Rob's brother. He would be able to keep up.

"I just hope she finds that ring soon," Paris muttered, almost beneath her breath. "There will be no peace in this house until she does."

Summer nodded numbly as Paris crossed the room and bent to slide a basket out from under the pastry bench. She lifted it, turning with a grace that marked most of her movements. "Here." Paris set the basket up on the worktable. "You go rinse the rinds at the well. I'll start the vinegar heating and get a fire going in the bake oven. I won't get to baking until after noon if I don't get started." Paris began stirring at the hearth fire, humming. Summer watched her slip a handful of rock salt from the bag near the hearth and spill it into the vinegar pot. Paris looked up. "Shoo!"

Summer turned and pushed the door open, then stood blinking in the sunlight as Letty came out of the great house. Letty hesitated, then approached, turning to let her wide skirt pass through the door.

Summer clutched the basket of watermelon rinds so tightly her fingers hurt. "Please return my sketchbook," she whispered. "Please, Letty. I have never done you any harm."

Letty shook her head. "Not until you confess."

"Confess?" Summer stared at her. "I haven't done anything."

Letty frowned. "Of course you did. You stole my mother's ring."

CHAPTER FIVE

"Letty?"

It was Mistress Weller, coming out the door, her face stern. She turned sideward as Letty had, her skirt hoops jouncing with her movements. She had changed into one of her better dresses, Summer realized, a bright yellow silk overskirt, the panniers that tied onto each hip draped with a sky-colored dimity. The underskirt was embroidered. These visitors meant something to her—something more than extending simple hospitality to neighbors. She had on her better wig, too, the long cascades of powdered curls brushing her shoulders.

"Letty, come here. And Summer, you stay close for a moment as well. When I am finished talking to Letty I have something to ask you."

Summer nodded respectfully, staring at the embroidery that edged Mistress Weller's hem. Paris had likely done the beautiful thread work. The seamstress Mistress Weller used was very good—except for embroidery.

Paris's needlework was so fine Master Weller sometimes hired her out. He had often said he wished he could divide Paris in two, half cook and half seamstress. Paris had smiled at the compliment, but Summer had overheard her later, wondering aloud to Myrna why she would want to work twice as hard for Master Weller. She never saw any of her hire-out wages, after all.

Mistress Weller was smoothing her skirts and bending down to speak to Letty. "We will soon be receiving Mr. Gellin and his English cousin. They will stay for tea, then go on to Calderfields. With your father gone to Court Day, the duties of host fall upon Rob. I shall want you and Anna to be presentable. Wear your wig, Letty, not a cap."

Summer glanced sidelong. Letty hated being presented. Anna loved it. She would play her flute or give a piece, reciting dramatically, delighted when the visitors applauded at the end. Letty usually blushed and stammered when the sharp-dressed gentlemen asked her questions.

"Have you seen Rob?"

Letty was shaking her head and Mistress Weller's eyes connected with Summer's.

"Have you?"

Summer tried not to look away. "He was talking to Mistress Anna in the parlor when I came past."

"Go on, please, Letty," Mistress Weller said evenly, turning to face her daughter. "*Dress!*"

Letty shot Summer a look, then turned quickly, her hoops pumping up and down as she ran the four or five steps to the door and jerked it open. Once the door had closed behind her, Mistress Weller turned fully around to fix her eyes on Summer again.

"What were you doing outside last night?"

Summer felt her cheeks warming. "I wanted to relight my candle," she managed.

Mistress Weller nodded, an exaggerated, impatient motion. "My husband told me as much. But *why?*"

"I was . . ." Summer began. The basket was heavy in her arms and she longed to set it down, to run, to escape Mistress Weller's piercing eyes. She wasn't sure what to say. She had ended up using the candle to change James's swaddling cloths. But that certainly wasn't the reason she had come out. She took a breath, meaning to tell Mistress Weller everything. "I heard crying," she began. "And I—"

"James woke you?" Mistress Weller interrupted. "That explains the wet swaddling so early this morning!" There was obvious relief in her voice. "Fisk said you'd either swaddled James faster than anyone had ever done, or you had done it in the night."

"He was wet through," Summer said carefully. "Bedraggled."

Mistress Weller was smiling now. "There's no reason to hide conscientious work, Summer. It was foolish to go out your window because you were afraid of being punished for opening the door. You will be certain not to do it ever again, won't you? We do not need foolishness now, what with my ring missing."

She reached out and patted Summer's cheek, then turned to go back in. Summer stepped aside to avoid the swooshing width of her skirt. Once the door closed she sighed and turned around slowly, staring at the walk. The wider tenth plank was easy to spot.

Summer flinched when the door banged open behind her. Zilpha came out of the great house, a basket of laundry balanced on her head. Swaying like a daisy in the gentle breeze, she smiled at Summer, then walked toward the washhouse.

Her nerves jangled, Summer set off toward the well, determined to get a good look beneath the plank as soon as she could without being caught at it. The last thing she needed was for someone to see her doing something odd, something suspicious.

"Good day to you, Summer!"

It was Dody, walking toward her with swinging steps that fluttered the tail of her long shirt. Her legs were scratched and scarred from the rough wood of the heavy milking buckets. She was smiling, as usual. She worked hard every day in the dairy, following Frieda's barked orders without ever complaining. Summer smiled broadly.

"What was all the fuss this morning?" Dody asked, falling into step beside Summer. She reached to take one of the basket handles and Summer let it swing down between them, sharing the weight.

"Someone stole a ring from Mistress Weller," Summer said, glancing to see Dody's reaction.

Her eyes went wide. "Stole?"

Summer nodded. "It's gone. She called the whole household together to tell us."

Dody lifted her chin to gesture toward the well. "That where you're going?"

Summer nodded. Dody shifted course, starting down the grassy incline below the springhouse. It was crisscrossed with paths leading from one outbuilding to another. Summer heard whistling from the smoke-house off to their right. "Toby is getting some meat for Marse Weller to carry in his saddle wallet," Dody told her. "Marse is off to Court Day with Master Kyler. Rob is staying here, I think?"

Summer nodded. "Mistress Weller said we were to have visitors at midday."

Dody frowned. "Who? Not a batch of fine ladies and gents, I hope. The last party used up a month of cheese."

Summer shook her head. "Two men, here for tea, then gone on their way. Miss Letty has to be presented." She picked her way down the increasingly muddy path, not daring to glance at Dody for fear of slipping until she got to the bottom.

Dody was smiling, a tight little smile. "Oh, she purely does hate being presented."

Summer nodded, then saw the little twinkle in Dody's eye and they both giggled.

"We are not being very kind," Summer said as they lifted the basket to the well bench together.

"Letty is often not very kind," Dody said very quietly.

Summer looked into Dody's dark eyes and grinned. "She most assuredly is not."

"Then sometimes, some folks are going to take pleasure in her little discomforts," Dody whispered, looking around. "She barely speaks to me now, Summer."

Summer didn't know what to say. She dropped the bucket down the well, giving the rope a sharp tug to one side to keep the bucket from floating upright on the water's surface. When she felt it sink, she waited a few seconds, then leaned out over the well to pull the rope hand over hand. Dody waited, watching, her eyes narrow.

"Who do you think did it?"

Summer shrugged. "I don't know. I thought about every one of us in the great house. Who would?"

"Anyone would *know* there'd be a big fuss," Dody said. "That ring belonged to Mistress Weller's mother, Fisk said."

Dody paused when Summer turned around with the full bucket to stare at her. "You already knew?"

"Fisk had to get something from Paris this morning. Lard I think, for his lye scalds. I was out rinsing milk buckets and we crossed paths."

Summer blinked, resolving to keep her lips closed about her missing diary. If she didn't, everyone on the plantation would know within an hour. "Who does Fisk think did it?" she whispered.

Dody tipped the rinds out on the well bench and shrugged. "If it was one of the slaves, there'll never be anywhere safe to trade or sell it. Anyone would know that no Negro could honestly come by such a thing."

"Nor anyone bound," Summer agreed.

Using wads of grass, they began scrubbing all the little plackets of soil from the watermelon rinds, sloshing the cleaned ones in the bucket to rinse.

"Frieda is honest, isn't she?" Summer asked. "I almost never talk to her."

"You wouldn't," Dody agreed, bending to get a fresh handful of grass. "She's never in the great house, hardly. Nor me, anymore." She scoured another curving piece of rind and rinsed it, a sad expression in her eyes. "Frieda came all the way from Germany to London, then clear across the ocean to Virginia. She had her two little sons with her—her husband had died. So she bound herself out to get here. Eighteen years bound."

Summer finished the last piece of rind. "I never knew she had sons—"

"She doesn't," Dody cut her off. "They both died first year after they came. Fever."

"Dear God," Summer breathed.

Dody dumped the water and they started placing the rinds back in the basket. "She told me she won't run out. She said she owes Marse Weller for three passages from London, fair and square."

Summer met Dody's eyes, understanding why she had told the story. Frieda was hardly suspect of stealing if her character demanded she work off the passage of two sons who no longer lived.

"She'll be thirty-nine," Dody breathed. "Maybe she won't live that long."

"I'll be twenty," Summer said, "when I come free. I can barely wait." She closed her mouth, looking into Dody's dark eyes. Then she blushed.

Dody arched her brows and tipped her head back. "And I'll be dead."

"Dody? Where are you, girl?" It was Frieda's clipped, shrill voice.

Dody kept her eyes on Summer. "You can manage that basket well enough, can't you?"

Summer nodded, feeling strange and sad. "I can. I'm sorry, Dody. I didn't mean to—"

Dody shook her head. "Truth's truth. Did you steal it?"

Summer had already turned away, starting back up the muddy path, but now she came back around, the basket tight against her chest. "No. Of course not!"

"That's not what Letty is saying," Dody whispered.

CHAPTER SIX

Summer was thunderstruck. "Letty told you that I—"

"She told others, not me. Don't ask me who, Summer."

Summer tried to hold Dody's eyes, but couldn't. She knew why. Dody didn't want to tell her where the accusation had come from. Her heart was aching as she started for the cookhouse. Had Letty told six other people and God Himself as well?

Summer clenched at the basket, fighting tears as she made her way up the hill past the springhouse. For a moment, she stood at the top of the rise, looking down at the garden.

She could see the silver green of the cabbage leaves and the slim spikes of the onions and celeriac. She loved working in the garden, out past the long hedge that hid the slave cabins from sight of the parlor windows. She had done more of it the year before, before James had been given into her care. Now most of the work was done by Ephrim and Fisk, when their other chores were finished.

Summer turned to go down the hill, knowing there was no choice. She stood outside the cookhouse door for a moment, wiping at her eyes with her sleeve, taking long breaths, determined that Paris would not be able to tell she was upset—or everyone would begin to think she was guilty. She arched her back against her stays, pulling her dress front straight. Only when she had taken four or five slow breaths and calmed down did she go inside.

Paris looked up from the hearth. "Are you well, child? You look flushed."

Summer nodded, kept nodding. "A little chilly maybe, from the well water."

Paris placed another small stack of wood on her vinegar-boiling fire—she had three separate fires going on the enormous hearth now. One licked at the base of the big kettle—she was starting the supper stew. "Summer?"

Summer tore her eyes from the flickering flames and focused on Paris's patient face. "You'd best go see whether the little one is awake or not. He's likely hungry again by now."

Ashamed that she had not thought of it herself, Summer set the basket down on the worktable with a startled thump. How could she have forgotten little James? She whirled around and started toward the door. "I'll be back after I fetch him out to Myrna," she said over her shoulder. "If he's not sleepy, I'll just bring the standing stool in here."

"That'll be fine," Paris said in her easy, calm voice.

Summer hurried out the door, a little out of breath, feeling very foolish indeed. She had not stolen anything. She had written in a sketchbook—a few pages of essays in imitation of Rob's assignments, and a few more of arithmetical studies. Beyond that were her diary entries, her thoughts and feelings at a day's end. . . .

Summer had just begun to feel a little better when she remembered an evening when she had been angry at Master Weller. Alone with little James, she had written of Master Weller's unfairness. She had once written of Anna's vanity as well, she realized, and any number of times, of Letty's selfishness.

Summer tried to recall everything she had ever written, her heart speeding up as she pushed open the great house door.

She could hear James crying the instant she entered. She hurried down the hall, passing Anna, who eyed her with distaste, her glare accusing Summer of neglecting her small charge.

"I was out helping Paris in the cookhouse," Summer murmured as she went by.

Anna made a sound of dismissal, and Summer

looked back to see her bending to adjust the great, oblong expanse of her hoops. It was only then that Summer realized that Anna was wearing a new dress, one she had never seen before, and the wig she saved for dances. At the door to her chamber, Summer looked once more, in time to see Anna sweeping her way through the wide parlor door.

The gown was a rich wine color with a deep gold ruching along the hem. The bodice and stomacher were a soft rose. Anna obviously wanted to impress someone today. One of the visitors? Perhaps the young English cousin was unmarried, handsome, and rich.

"I am so sorry, little James," Summer said as she came in. "I have been distracted," she went on, crooning to him as she crossed the room.

At the first sound of her voice, James quieted a bit, his cries softening even more as she came close. He wriggled within his swaddling and she quickly passed her hands over the wrappings, checking the straight pins to make sure none of them had angled into his tender skin.

"You are just hungry again," Summer murmured to him as she walked him back and forth until his crying fell into little sniffles. "I'll carry you to Myrna, but you have to promise me that you won't start shrieking like a lost soul on the way down the passage. Mistress Weller is expecting company any time now."

James made a gurgling sound as she cradled him in her arms and let him suck on the side of her thumb.

"We'll have to go out the cookhouse door," she explained to him in the same soothing voice. "The quickest way is straight through the parlor, then out the front, but we can't do that today."

Once Summer started down the passage, she walked as fast as she could, her eyes on the wide parlor door straight ahead, her ears alert for the sound of unfamiliar voices. James stayed still in her arms and he made almost no noise at all as she turned right and emerged outside, glancing only once at the tenth plank before she turned again, climbing the steps up onto the long porch that ran along the back of the great house.

Summer went down the steps at the far end and rounded the end of the building, skirting Paris's herb bed. She headed across the wide yard toward the tall hedge that stood between it and the row of slave cabins. There were several places to pass through the hedge by ducking or squeezing, but the only real gate was in the center—straight out from the parlor doors. Summer headed toward it and slipped through, then slowed her steps a little, more comfortable out of sight of the wide parlor windows.

As she approached the line of low-roofed log cabins, she saw Myrna standing in the last doorway, smoking her pipe. She smiled as Summer got closer.

"Is our baby boy crying again?"

Summer nodded, extending James toward her. Myrna clamped her pipe between her teeth and took him.

"I'll just wait," Summer said, hesitating a moment, standing on the rough threshold looking into Myrna's cabin. The window had curtains made of old seed bags, tucked and flounced like the bottom of a skirt.

"Did you see . . ." Summer began, then stopped.

"See what?" Myrna asked her, loosening her blouse to nurse.

Summer hesitated. "I don't know. Anything odd?"

"I'm not sure what you mean, honey," Myrna said evenly.

"Anything about the ring," Summer managed.

Myrna shook her head. "Toby claims he saw Miss Anna out here this morning, but I don't think he really did."

"Would Toby make it up?"

Myrna shrugged. "Why would she come out here? Why wouldn't she just hide it in her room or somewhere closer. I hope it isn't so," she added, sitting down in the nursing chair. "With all my heart and soul, I hope it isn't. They'll pick one of us to whip or sell or worse, if they can think of worse. Especially if they find it out here by the cabins."

Summer felt her stomach tighten. "Letty told someone I did it," she ventured.

Myrna made a little huffing sound of disgust. "And why would you? Why would I or anyone else here? So we could get sold down the river or cut with the lash or ducked in water till we burst?"

Summer shook her head. It really didn't make any sense.

"And who would chance going into Mistress Weller's chambers?" Myrna asked. She set down her pipe and rubbed James on the back as he nursed.

Summer nodded. It was true. "The only ones who ever go in and out of her chamber—"

"Are Toby or Fisk or Zilpha," Myrna finished for her.

"Or her daughters." Summer paused. Toby was the one who said he had seen Anna. Maybe he was just trying to make Anna look guilty—when he was the one after all.

"Toby might be able to sell a ring like that," Summer whispered, realizing it was true. "He goes everywhere with Rob now, to Court Day, visiting, dances, up to the cockfights up at Lancaster's. There are strollers there, Rob says, men nobody even knows where they are from, much less anything about their families."

Myrna was nodding, a thoughtful look on her face. "But I don't think Toby would. Nor Zilpha. She lives for church every Sunday—it'd go against that. Nor Fisk, of course. Fisk won't hardly take his share of a hoecake. And Toby prizes his position in the great house."

Summer reached out as Myrna handed James back to her. She propped him against her shoulder and patted his back as she spoke. "You're right. Toby isn't foolish enough. But someone might believe that I did it," she added, and felt anger rising inside her.

Myrna made a clucking sound like the one Paris often made. "Possibly. Indentureds are different," Myrna said. "Something small like a ring, you hide for eight or nine years. Then once you're free—"

"But Letty is lying," Summer blurted out.

Myrna nodded, then shrugged helplessly. She was silent a moment and when she spoke, her voice was matter-of-fact. "Won't be long until they are giving this little fellow his first set of stays and a long coat," she said slowly and carefully, tugging at James's white linen shirt. She was changing the subject and Summer knew why. It was dangerous for Myrna to talk about the family—any of them.

Summer closed her mouth hard, pressing her lips together. She shifted James on her shoulder, patting a little harder, until he burped.

"That works, doesn't it?" Myrna asked.

Summer smiled. "He doesn't get a bad stomach nearly so often since you showed me." She looked around. "I had best get back. Paris is waiting on me for help at pickling."

Myrna crossed the swept dirt floor to look down at her own baby where he lay in his drawer-box cradle, then she followed Summer back out the door.

Summer blinked, her eyes watering. The sunlight seemed impossibly bright after the darkness inside the little cabin. As they stepped over the half-round log that served as a threshold, a chicken scooted past them, her head low as she bustled by. Myrna laughed. "She lays her egg on my hearth every morning. One less I have to go hunt for. She's welcome by me!"

Summer smiled again and nodded. Myrna stretched and yawned. "I was up half the night with my baby. He's starting to teethe." An anxious look crossed her face.

"He's strong and healthy, Myrna," Summer said quickly. "I'm sure he'll be fine."

Myrna nodded. "My last boy died at three. I pray every day that this one lives."

Summer looked aside. She remembered Myrna's last little boy, a laughing, merry child who had sickened with a terrible fever that just burned his life right up. Summer hitched James a little higher in her arms.

"That's where Toby said he saw Mistress Anna," Myrna was saying, her voice nearly a whisper. She pointed to a pile of leaves and brush—stacked up from the apple prunings. Beyond the pile, Summer saw the lines of old apple trees, planted by Master Weller's father. "I wish I could think what in blue heaven she was about out there. Maybe she was just picking up a few twigs for those bouquets of hers."

Summer stared. Of course. Anna was forever arranging flowers and dried plants in the big vases in the parlor. But why had she been out so early?

"You best get along back to the cookhouse," Myrna said. "And I'd best get back to my small wheel." She pointed at the bundles of unspun hemp fiber lying beside her door.

"Good-bye," Summer said. She jiggled James and he smiled his toothless smile. "I'll bring him out again before dinner."

Myrna nodded as she turned back to the cabin. "I'll be here."

As Summer started out for the great house, James was gurgling and babbling against her shoulder. When she came to the opening in the hedge, she hesitated. There were two horses she didn't recognize at the tether posts in front of the big double parlor doors. The guests had arrived. That meant everyone would be staying in the parlor, at least for a little while. Summer half turned and looked back out toward the orchard. Then, on an impulse, she turned and hurried toward it.

James was delighted to be going somewhere new.

His eyes sparkled as she set him down carefully on some soft grass in the shade. He gurgled and cooed the whole time she was poking at the brush, lifting one rotten limb, then another. She squatted, staring at the dirt. There were no signs of digging that she could see.

The pinging of a hammer brought Summer upright and she whirled to see Ephrim seated on a roof with his back to her, bent over his work. Fisk was below, standing at the base of a ladder propped up against the side of the end cabin. And he was staring straight at her.

Summer snatched James up and tried to walk in a natural fashion, her cheeks flaming and her heart thudding inside her chest. Her thoughts roared within her mind, most of them chiding her, calling her a fool. She made her way along the hedge, back to the stone path, and she went through the opening without looking back.

Just then, the doors opened and Toby came out, glancing first this way, then that. Summer stumbled to a stop and stepped back through the opening and quickly to one side. She leaned against the hedge, the stiff branches pricking at her. One glance assured her that the first three cabins kept Fisk and Ephrim from seeing her here.

Summer let her breath out slowly, then crouched, holding James gently against her chest. Her stays digging into her abdomen, she stayed low, peeking around the hedge to watch.

Toby stepped off the wide front porch and approached the horses. He patted one, then the other, then he did something that made no sense at all to Summer. Glancing back behind himself once more, he strode away from the great house, walking as fast as a man can walk without breaking into a run.

Toby strode to the far end of the yard, then stooped to go through the hedge—like the field boys did when they got caught running around the great house by Master Weller.

Summer stepped through the opening in the hedge and peeked—looking the other way now, back toward the cabins. Toby was walking a straight course, not looking to either side. Summer half crouched again, trying to see if he veered left—out toward the pile of limbs and brush. The sudden sound of voices behind her made Summer whirl around, catching her hem beneath her bare foot and stumbling a little. James made a little sound of surprise, then began to cry.

CHAPTER SEVEN

The wide parlor doors were opening. Summer barely had time to soothe James, apologizing for startling him. She took one step toward the great house, hoisting James up higher on her hip. His face puckered up and she was afraid for a second that he was going to start crying again.

"Summer?" Mistress Weller's voice startled her and she looked up, across the yard. They were standing on the porch now. The two gentlemen visitors were holding their hats and gloves. Off to one side Letty stood awkwardly. As graceful as a bird, Anna was stepping off the porch, her hoops floating a lively dance around her legs as she walked toward Summer. She tipped her hoops to one side, lifting her skirt to show up a quick glimpse of her petticoat, a flash of the shape of her leg beneath it.

"Hand James to me," she said as she got close. "Mama wants to show him to Mr. Gellin and Mr. Elliot."

Summer let Anna take James, then stood, uncertain

what to do until Anna glanced back over her shoulder. "Wait here."

Summer nodded, even though Anna had turned away and couldn't see her. Then she smoothed her skirt, suddenly conscious of how small it had gotten for her over the past half year. The linen was clean, Fisk saw to that with his boiling salts and Paris's strong lye soap—but all the little frayed ends of threads seemed to stand out in the sunlight. Anna's wide and shining skirt flounced once, rippling beautifully as she stepped back up onto the porch, holding James.

The visitors both came forward, smiling good naturedly. One, an older man with graying hair, touched James's cheek and spoke to Mistress Weller, saying something that made her laugh. Then the younger man approached.

He was perhaps twenty, and his dark brown hair was full and wavy. Anna swayed and sidled within the great oval bell of her skirts and Summer saw her looking at the man sidelong, from beneath her lashes, as she held her little brother up for his inspection.

Mistress Weller laughed, a genteel, tinkling sound, as James began to squirm and cry. "Whatever are you doing to my son to spoil him so," she accused teasingly, making a motion with her hand that Summer knew was her cue. She came forward diffidently, waiting for Anna to stop exchanging glances with the young man before she turned around.

"He's *wet*, Summer," she whispered, crinkling her nose prettily, handing him back to Summer.

"I am used to it," Summer assured her.

Anna smiled, dimpling her cheeks. "I hope to have a child-nurse as good as you for my family," she said kindly, glancing back toward the young man and smiling.

Summer nodded, unable to think of any good answer for Anna's compliment. Though she was almost always civil and polite, Anna usually spoke to slaves and servants only to criticize gently. All Summer wanted was to get away, to go back into the cookhouse with Paris where she was not so acutely conscious of her plain skirts and her frayed hem. She looked up at Mistress Weller.

"Thank you, Summer," Mistress Weller called to her in an overloud, overbright voice. She made her little shooing motion with her hand. Summer nodded respectfully and walked away, realizing only after she had gone a half dozen steps that she might as well have gone through the parlor this time—everyone was out on the porch anyway. Feeling foolish, she kept going, hoping that no one would point out her silliness.

Summer exhaled in relief as she rounded the corner of the great house without anyone calling her back. She walked just wide enough to miss the herb bed. Paris's lavender was in full bloom, the knobby little purple blooms on short, straight spikes.

For a moment, Summer just walked a little more slowly, shifting James's weight from one hip to the other, then she lifted her chin and looked past the springhouse to the cow barn. There was a little rill of smoke coming out of the washhouse chimney, she noticed. Fisk was back in the washhouse now.

Summer hurried a little, trying to put her mind back on everyday thoughts. She had to change James's swaddling, then get back to the cookhouse before Paris had finished with the pickling. Paris was kind about teaching her. Someday, she would have to find employment as a housekeeper or a cook, and she wanted to be very good at it.

Summer took a deep breath. As it usually did, the thought of being free, of having a little money of her own, excited her and scared her. Only seven years away now, she thought, and felt another chill go down her spine. Today her thoughts all seemed gloomy and her excitement gave way to worries.

Would she be able to support herself if she could not find a man she respected and liked enough to have as a husband? Master Weller told them all the time about the almshouses in the New England colonies and how the poor and destitute were given just enough to eat and worked like plow mules for their keep. He usually told them about the almshouses when he was worried about someone running off, Summer knew, but Paris had heard much the same thing. Many runaways ended up starving in the woods.

Anna would find a prosperous husband, Summer thought suddenly, and so would Letty, even as shy as she was. Master Weller would give them both generous marriage settlements—enough to attract men of good standing.

Summer tried to imagine her own husband. Maybe he would be a tutor like Thomas Kyler, or a someone who owned a small shop in Williamsburg or Charleston. She smiled, thinking about it. She could have ribbons for her hair, perhaps, plenty to eat most of the time, and children of her own. That would be enough. If only this business about the ring would end.

Summer hurried down the hall, changed James's swaddling and then picked him up, grabbing the standing stool with her free hand. As she passed close to the parlor door, she heard peals of ladylike laughter, then the slower, deeper chuckling of a man. So the guests hadn't left yet. Anna was charming this visitor, no doubt about it.

"That took longer than I thought it would," Paris commented as Summer came through the door. "I've been waiting on you."

Summer set down the standing stool and held James, watching as Paris swung the pot crane, moving the vinegar kettle away from the fire. The frothy bubbles on top subsided instantly, but it kept simmering. The pot was copper—iron soured vinegar and turned the rind—or anything else—blackish, Summer knew.

For the first time in hours, Summer felt solid and real, and she knew it was Paris's calm kindness that made her feel that way. "Thank you for teaching me to cook and keep," Summer said aloud. Paris smiled and dipped a little curtsy. Summer gave her one back. They laughed together.

There were four fires in the hearth now, and Summer saw little tendrils of smoke coming out of the bake oven. A roasting kitchen stood before the biggest fire and Summer could smell meat cooking.

Summer positioned the standing stool near the hearth, but not so close that James could be pushed into the flames by accident. Mistress Weller had told her awful stories that would be in her heart forever about babies burned in hearth fires.

"You see where he is?" she asked Paris, just to make sure.

"That's fine, that's fine," Paris answered her. "I don't need to get down to that end for quite a long time. That last pot is just what's left of the venison haunch. Flies got to it and it's full of maggots. I'm boiling it for tallow."

Summer nodded.

"Did Myrna say anything about the ring?" Paris asked abruptly.

Summer kissed the top of James's head, then straightened up to stare at her. "I thought you said that if I had nothing to do with it I shouldn't think about it."

Paris was shrugging. "Toby was back in here, asking where you were, then if I had seen Letty. He's afraid Mistress must be thinking it was him, since he can go into the bedchambers in his work."

"He was on his way out to the cabins a few minutes ago," Summer said.

Paris wrinkled her brow. "With Rob?"

Summer shook her head. "I didn't see Rob. The rest came out on the porch to look at James."

Paris frowned. "Anna asked me to make up some punch for the guests. I crushed some of those early peaches into the new cider, then I had Zilpha carry it in on the tray. I caught sight of Rob in the parlor then."

Summer understood what she was saying. If Rob was in the house, preoccupied with company, no one was likely to care if Toby slipped away for a few minutes.

"Maybe he went to see what Anna hid out there this morning," Summer said quietly. "If he could find the ring—that wouldn't be like stealing, would it?"

"What he'd do is just put it back," Paris said sternly. "He sure wouldn't expect Mistress to believe he'd just all of a sudden found it. She'd think he had stolen it, then got scared."

Summer nodded. "I just wish we could all stop worrying about what was going to happen."

Paris pulled open the door on the back of the roasting kitchen and used a ladle to baste the meat from the catchbasin. Then she closed the door, the tin clanking. "Toby was right about Mistress Weller wanting someone besides her children to be blamed. She has never cared much for her babies since she lost the two after Collier. Then a third one died small, too, the one between Letty and James. But once they grow up a little, she lets herself love them. And then she is as proud and fierce as a mother hen. Mistress Anna is her joy."

"Anna was flirting with the young man," Summer whispered, to take the bleak look from Paris's face.

Paris's face softened. "Really? And was he flirting back?"

"It looked like it to me," Summer told her. "They kept looking at each other and Miss Anna was as flushed as a rose."

Paris smiled and sighed, putting her hands on her hips. "Maybe everything will be all right. Let's stop thinking the worst. Would you mind running for some lavender down at the end of the house? I want to pepper up these rinds a little."

"You'll keep an eye on James?"

Paris nodded. "Of course. James and I are friends." She reached out one finger to touch his cheek. "Aren't we, little Marse?"

He wriggled, but the swaddling cloths held him upright and rigid. He made a cooing sound and Paris made it back at him. He smiled, watching her face. "Go on, Summer," she said without looking up. "Leave the door open. It's getting warm in here. And see if you can get back here quick this time. I had better have a company supper in mind in case Anna's visitor decides to stay."

Summer hurried back out into the sunshine and followed the planked walk to the porch steps. She could hear voices in the parlor as she passed its curtained windows on her way to the lavender bed. She picked the flowers quickly, laying each down carefully—Paris had told her that crushing the petals dissipated the spicy flavor. Once she had enough, she gathered them up gently and started back.

As she came around the corner of the house, walking fast to pass the parlor windows as quickly as she could, Summer caught a glimpse of Letty—her best wig on now and all dressed up, disappearing into the washhouse. Summer stopped and stood still, surprised. When did Letty ever go to the washhouse? And why would she go out there today, dressed for company? To talk to Fisk?

Summer watched the washhouse door, expecting Letty to come right back out, through telling Fisk what she needed to tell him. But the seconds ticked past and turned into a minute, then two. Letty was still inside. Summer tried to recall a single time when Letty had said more to Fisk than to ask him to change her linens or to tell him she had spilled something on a shift that needed vinegar or extra time spread out in the sun. She couldn't.

Summer bit her lip. Fisk had seen her, out by the orchard. He had seen her scratching around at the dirt. Would he tell Letty that? Had anyone told Letty about Anna? Summer stood watching the washhouse door, knowing she should move, should not be caught standing and staring when Letty did reappear.

"Summer?"

It was Paris's voice, a little perturbed, from inside the cookhouse.

"Coming!" Summer called back, managing to free her feet from the porch planks at last as she almost ran toward the cookhouse door.

Summer felt strange and frightened as she came out from under the roof eaves and stepped down from the porch, then up again, onto the plank walk. Nothing made any sense at all. And everything felt unsettled and dangerous. Someone was going to get hurt, just as surely as if all this was a lightning storm or a rising creek close to the house. Someone would be hurt—it was just a matter of finding out who, and how badly.

CHAPTER EIGHT

"You are slow as a snail today, child," Paris scolded as Summer came in the door.

"I saw Letty on the way back."

Paris took the lavender and placed the flowers on her worktable. She picked up one of her knives and began trimming away the coarse, squarish stems. "And what was our Missy Letty doing?"

"I don't know," Summer admitted. She went to the standing stool and touched James's head, then his shoulder. His soft linen shirt was pretty hot. His cheeks were a little pink, too, so she picked him up, stool and all, and resettled him another arm's length from the hearth. He sagged against the side of the standing stool, but he did not cry or fuss.

"Miss Summer?" The voice was brusque.

"Yes?" she answered, spinning around.

It was Zilpha, standing in the doorway. Her hands were on her hips, and she looked stern. "Mistress Weller asks to see you in the parlor."

Summer swallowed, her throat tightening. "Now?"

"She said to tell you that she wanted to see you in the parlor," Zilpha repeated.

Summer glanced at Paris, raising her hands, palms up.

"I'll see to James," Paris said.

Zilpha waited as Paris gave Summer a quick hug, then stepped back. As Summer went up the board-walk and pulled open the heavy door, she could hear Zilpha talking and she longed to go back out and listen. Zilpha had been indoors since morning. If there was anything more to be known, she would know it.

The passageway seemed dark after the sun and she paused after pulling the door closed to let her eyes get used to it.

"Summer? Is that you?" It was Rob, coming out the parlor door. "Mother wanted to show the gentleman that you can write well enough," he explained, coming toward her. His voice was warm, friendly. "She's got them talking about whether a tutor is needed for a daughter. Seems Mr. Gellin is wondering about his daughter Amy and—"

"Is that Summer?" Mistress Weller's voice was a little shrill. "Just bring her in, Rob, please?"

"Yes, Mother," Rob called back. He gestured for Summer to follow. She did, smoothing her apron nervously, her feet heavy with dread.

"Here she is," Mistress Weller sang out as she

came in. "Our little Summer." She looked up. "Paper and quill, Toby?"

Summer glanced aside. Toby had come back in. Had he finished whatever his errand had been out by the cabins? He was opening the little escritoire that stood in the corner of the room nearest the door.

"Just seat yourself at the desk, Summer," Mistress Weller said in a kindly voice. "We'll all just gather around you there."

Summer walked on wooden legs to the straight-backed chair and sank into it. The two gentlemen were getting up. The older man offered his arm to Mistress Weller. The younger man escorted Anna across the room to stand behind the chair. Anna and her mother turned sideward so their wide skirts would not hold the gentlemen too far away to see.

"Write your name," Mistress Weller commanded.

Summer took up the quill, dipped it in the ink pot, and scratched out her name. Her hand was trembling, even though there was nothing wrong with writing her name. They all knew she could write, after all—they knew she wrote letters to home. It was just that Mistress Weller had no idea how well she could write, how many hours she had practiced. No one did, unless they had seen the sketchbook that had become her diary.

"Now write this sentence," Anna said in a bright voice, as though this was a new parlor game and more fun than any of the old ones. "The horse stood wait-ing for its master."

Summer glanced up at Mistress Weller, who nodded. "Can you?"

Summer nodded and began, slowly and painstakingly because her fingers were clumsy with anxiety and because she kept glancing toward the door. Maybe Letty had no idea she was here. But what would happen when Letty walked back in?

Summer finished and set the quill back in the ink pot. If Mistress Weller asked for anything more, she would plead fatigue, pretend that her mind was tired from this much.

"See, Mother?" Rob exclaimed. "I told you she had a beautiful hand. And I see her listening when Mr. Kyler is lecturing me. I'll bet she could repeat much of what he has said—"

"Repeat is not to say understand," Anna inter-jected.

Summer glanced at her, then beyond her, to Toby. He was handing the younger man something. Something small that passed between them quickly, then was pocketed. Summer stared, but neither one looked nervous or secretive at all. The young man smiled. "You win the wager, Toby. I did not think it possible."

"If a girl can manage to write this well with almost no direct instruction," the older man was saying, "how quickly would she learn if a tutor were hired for her?" He touched his wig to adjust it. "Too quickly, perhaps. I do not mean to endanger my little Amy by overtaxing her mind."

"You are a good and loving father," Mistress Weller said approvingly. "Learning is a danger for a girl, nothing less. My husband would never allow either of our daughters to risk their sanity and serenity with a man's education." She touched her wig with careful fingertips.

"Write this, Summer," Rob was saying. "A servant's duty to his master is as man's duty to God." Summer hesitated and Rob instantly smiled. "You can do it easily, can't you? You write your letters home, I know."

Summer was frightened and her thoughts whirled. Had she learned too much? Would it hurt her mind if she kept it up? Had it already?

"I think you are clever to question the value of instruction at dancing and drawing," Mistress Weller was saying to the older man. "Girls need most to learn how to run a household. They must save and make do and stretch their husband's stores—keep his wealth from disappearing into thin air. Pretty accomplishments are nothing to that."

Summer turned to look over her shoulder. Anna was still looking up at the younger man, absorbing his words like dry ground absorbs rain.

Summer began to stand up, but Rob put his

hand on her shoulder. "Give her a simple sum, Mother. Let's see if she can cipher."

"I really ought to get back to James," Summer said quietly.

"This has all been quite impressive," the older man was saying to Mistress Weller, waving his hand back and forth in a vague gesture. "And with no formal tutoring at all. Well! It does give me pause, and I thank you for the demonstration."

Mistress Weller gave Summer a little pat of dismissal on her shoulder, then walked, with her guests just behind her, back across the room. The men remained on their feet and the older man began thanking Mistress Weller for her hospitality. Anna stood with her chin high and her back very straight, staring at Summer for a moment. The low-cut bodice of her gown showed off the milky white skin of her throat. Her stays reduced her waist to a slender stem.

Anna looked so beautiful, Summer thought, as she slid the chair back and stood up to go. The young man was staring at her. Summer looked down at her dress again, noticing every tawdry seam, every inelegant wrinkle and pucker. Anna half turned, a motion that sent her skirts rustling into motion. "You may go now, Summer," she said in a perfectly kind tone.

Summer nodded and walked out of the room on wobbly legs. There had been nothing odd in Anna's expression—so perhaps Letty had not shown her the sketchbook at all. But if Letty was telling Dody and Myrna and everyone else that Summer had stolen the ring, why hadn't Letty told Rob and her mother and sister? Maybe she was hoping someone else would.

Once out in the dark passageway, Summer paused, then started for her room, trying to collect her thoughts.

"I insist that you come," Letty's voice suddenly rang out behind her. Summer turned, then backed up as bright sunlight streamed in, making her squint. Letty was opening the door, stepping into the passageway, moving aside to let someone else come in behind her. Summer saw Fisk's uneven silhouette, one shoulder canted higher than the other to compensate for his limp.

"You have nothing to be afraid of, Fisk," Letty was saying quietly, her back to Summer.

Summer stood motionless, then turned and fled a few steps, shrinking backward into the doorway of the storage room. She turned the door handle downward, slowly, without a sound, and slipped inside. Leaving the door ajar a few inches, she trembled as she peeked out.

Letty was fidgeting and Fisk looked miserable. "You had nothing to do with it. My father will not punish you," Letty said sharply.

"I jes' want to get on back to my work, Mistress,"

Fisk answered awkwardly. "I tol' Master Weller I'd be done with his shirts and collars by the time he got back tonight and I—"

"I just want you to tell my mother what you saw," Letty insisted.

"I didn't see nothin' important," Fisk muttered, and Summer heard Letty sigh.

"You said you saw Summer MacCleary out in the dairy today. That's no part of her duties, as well you know. And she was poking through the woodpile, you said."

Fisk bridled. "I can't see no harm in neither one, Mistress. You just asked had I seen anything unusual."

Letty looked up and Summer stiffened, narrowing the small gap in the door even more. Her heart was thudding in her chest.

"Mister Gellin and his cousin are still here," Letty said, and her voice was so close and so clear that Summer peeked out again. Letty was standing not more than an arm's length or two from her. Fisk was beside her, his big knotted hands clasped together. "Just wait here, down at this end, out of the way, Fisk. I'll call you." Letty walked in mincing, proper little steps back toward the parlor.

Summer stood very still, breathing in trembly little bursts. If she came sly-booting out of the store-room now, Fisk would start to believe Letty was right about her. Summer closed her eyes, fighting back tears.

CHAPTER NINE

When Letty finally came back, Fisk tried again to persuade her to let him leave. "Just come in now," Letty cut him off. "My mother is waiting."

As Fisk limped past the linen closet door, Summer held her breath, counting to ten once they were out of sight, then to ten again for good measure, before she opened the door wide enough to see into the passage. The parlor door at the other end had been pulled shut. She came out of the storeroom running.

"What happened?" Paris exploded at her as she came into the cookhouse.

Barely managing not to cry, Summer picked James up out of the standing stool and paced back and forth with him in her arms. She hugged him close, his warm cheek against her own.

"What happened in there?" Paris asked in a gentler voice.

Dabbing at her eyes with the edge of her apron,

Summer decided to explain everything, including her diary and how Letty had stolen it. She told Paris how Letty had locked her out the night before, about Master Weller letting her in, and about overhearing Fisk and Letty in the passageway.

"And you heard her say all that to Fisk?" Paris asked, when Summer was finished. "You haven't made a single thing up?"

Summer shook her head. "No. She is going to accuse me of taking the ring. I know it. Because I went out to the dairy and because I looked around by the orchard woodpile."

"And why did you? What in the world were you doing?"

"Toby saw Anna out there just after dawn," Summer told her. "That's what he wanted to tell you this morning."

"Oh, my, oh, my." Paris smoothed her apron front with the flats of her palms, then picked up a poker and stirred the smallest fire. "What have you done to make Letty so angry with you?"

Summer tried to think. "We don't play very much together anymore because of James. And Mistress Weller is trying to get Letty to spend more of her time learning how to manage the household—not just pretending tea parties and dances as we did for so long. She is the one who sent Letty out to help with the soapmaking."

"Letty can't possibly expect you two to remain friends forever."

Summer shrugged. "I suppose not. But she is acting like an enemy. Could she actually think that I did it? She knows I am honest, Paris."

"Sometimes, things make no sense." Paris wiped her forehead with the back of her hand. It was getting on toward noon and the cookhouse was warming up. "Another few hours," she said evenly, "and it'll be like fixing supper in Hades." She forced a chuckle at her own joke, then frowned again. "I wish I knew how to help you."

Summer tried to smile at her. "I know you would if you could, Paris. And I thank you for that." James was beginning to fuss and Summer patted his back. He was probably getting hungry again.

"Missy Summer?"

The sound of Fisk's polite voice spun her around, startled.

"Missus Weller would like you to come speak with her, she said."

"Oh, my," Paris breathed.

Summer felt her hands begin to tremble. James sensed her uneasiness and his whimpering got louder.

"Did she say why?" Paris asked Fisk.

He ducked his head. "No. But it's got to do with that ring. Missy Letty made me tell about seeing you at the dairy and—"

"I know," Summer said quickly to spare him repeating it. "It's not your fault, Fisk. And I didn't steal it."

He nodded. His face was compressed with pain most of the time. Now, his concern for her shone in his eyes as well. He gave her a little half bow of sympathy and turned awkwardly, limping back along the planked walk.

"I did not steal that ring," Summer said, looking heavenward. "I did not!"

Paris shook her head. "God knows what's true without anyone telling Him—and I already believe you. It's Mistress Weller you need to convince."

Summer jiggled James up and down. His crying was louder now. "He's hungry, Paris. Would you—"

"I'll fetch him out to Myrna for you," Paris interrupted her.

Summer nodded and handed James to her. His cheeks were flushed. He struggled against his swaddling and began to cry. "Check his pins?" she said, glancing back at the door.

"Of course I will," Paris reassured her.

Summer turned and walked to the door, then looked back over her shoulder. "I'm frightened."

"God bless you," Paris said very softly.

Summer managed a smile of thanks.

They were all lined up in the parlor when she walked in—standing side by side and watching her. In a row like this, they were like colorful birds in their fine clothes, their bright silks grand and shimmering in the light from the front windows. The carpet shone deep reds and blues beneath their feet.

"Come in, please, Summer," Mistress Weller said. She was at one end of the row, Rob at the other. Letty and Anna stood between them.

Summer took one step inside the door and waited beside the little desk.

"No," Mistress Weller said sternly. "Come here—right here in front of me."

Summer stepped from the planked floor onto the thick carpet, and, as always, it felt too soft—unfamiliar and unsettling beneath her feet. She walked slowly, feeling almost dizzy with dread.

"Letty has told me several things, which make me believe that you are the one we have been hoping would come forward."

Summer kept silent as her heart faltered. She pressed her lips together. She tried to look straight in Mistress Weller's eyes. She did not want Mistress Weller to think her insolent—only innocent.

"I have not come forward," she began in a wavery voice—then had to stop and clear her throat. "I have not come forward because I did nothing wrong."

Letty turned to her mother. "She is lying."

Summer stared at Letty. Her chin was set and Summer could see a vein pulsing in her throat. She looked like someone who was afraid, not angry.

"Summer?"

Mistress Weller's voice was sharp, demanding. "I want my ring back, Summer. Not only is it valuable, I value it as a keepsake from my grandmother."

Summer squared her shoulders. "I didn't take the ring. I have never *seen* the ring."

Mistress Weller was watching her closely now, her eyes pinched and her mouth in a severe, straight line. Summer swallowed awkwardly, trying not to look aside or down at her feet. She curled her bare toes against the soft carpet and waited for Mistress Weller to say something. It seemed to take forever.

"Where is James?"

Summer gestured toward the cabins. "Paris carried him out to Myrna."

Mistress Weller nodded. "Go to your room now, Summer. I will send for you."

Summer stood still for a few seconds, stunned by the icy authority in Mistress Weller's voice. Then she left the parlor, the planks cool and hard as she walked down the passage. She closed the door behind herself, then sat on the edge of her cot.

Maybe Master Weller would sell her contract now. If he did, and she wound up with a cruel master who beat her or who didn't feed her enough, she would run away. Even if they sent the dogs after her—

"Don't be stupid," she told herself, speaking aloud. "You couldn't travel alone and anyone who saw you would know you for exactly what you are—an indentured girl run off from her master." Summer felt tears stinging at her eyes. Letty did not understand what she was doing. Why should she? No one could ever buy or sell *her*.

For a moment, Summer imagined herself in a flounced overskirt of bright canary yellow silk edged in Mechlin lace, with a ruffled dimity underskirt flaring from her ankles, her shoulders bare, white and perfect like Anna's. There would be a fair-haired young man someday and—

"Don't be stupid," she told herself again. "A gown like that costs more hard money than you will ever see in your life."

Voices in the passage ended her thoughts and she got up to open her door just a crack to listen. She heard Rob saying something, then Anna's voice, then Mistress Weller's clipped tone. Then, as she listened, she could hear Myrna talking.

Summer pressed her ear close to the little crack in the door. Why was Myrna in the great house? Had she brought James in? The voices jumbled together and she could only pick out phrases here and there.

"She was out there all right." That was Letty.

"No proof of any kind," Rob was saying.

". . . best to wait for your father to come home." That was Mistress Weller.

Then Rob's voice came to Summer, clear and

distinct. "We could take her out there. If we find something, she might confess. Or, if we find nothing, and she seems innocent. . . . "

They all fell silent. After a moment, Summer heard footsteps coming down the passageway. They paused before her door.

CHAPTER TEN

The trek to the woodpile made treacherous walking for Mistress Weller and her daughters in their heeled slippers and bobbing skirts. Letty went most slowly, turning sideways to follow her sister through the gap in the hedge. Anna's face was pale, and Summer watched her closely. Whatever was out at the woodpile, Anna was the one who knew what it was and where. It was hard to believe that serious, responsible Anna would have taken her mother's ring, but what else would she have been hiding out here?

As Mistress Weller turned toward the orchard, Summer followed her swaying silk skirts. There was a wild feeling in her heart, as though she could suddenly fly straight up and leave them all behind, like a flushed dove. She imagined soaring over the cabins, disappearing, leaving them all to jabber and wonder. The sound of Ephrim's hammer disrupted her thoughts. She could see him on the roof of the second cabin now. Fisk was nowhere to be seen.

Myrna had put James in his cradle and then followed the procession, keeping a little ways back so she could turn off and head for her own cabin. When Summer turned to glance at her, she made a tiny apologetic wave of her hand, but then quickly turned her head, as though she hadn't seen Summer's glance at all.

"Summer?" Mistress Weller asked as they got closer to the untidy stack of limbs and brush. "Where is my ring? Did you hide it out here?"

Summer shook her head.

Mistress Weller arched her brows. "Letty and Myrna and Fisk saw you out here, rooting around." She glanced back at the row of cabins. Myrna hadn't seen her, had she? Or Letty? Myrna might have.

"Where is my ring? Do you know?" Mistress Weller asked again.

"Don't be afraid, Summer," Rob said, coming closer, watching her face closely. "Just answer Mother's question, and everything will be all right."

Summer met his eyes and realized that he believed it. He had never learned fear and no one else's made any sense to him.

"Why were you out here?" Rob went on, patiently. "What were you doing? Even if it seems silly to you, or it's something embarrassing, just say it and we can be finished."

He didn't believe she had done it, Summer thought, and he was urging her to defend herself.

Knowing that Rob believed her innocent warmed her heart a little. Summer looked past him at Letty. She was smiling, a strained, tight little smile. Anna was still pale. As Summer watched her, her eyes flickered over to one corner of the woodpile, then away.

"If you have done nothing wrong, then you have nothing to fear from my father," Rob was saying, loudly, clearly, as if he was talking to a person who didn't have all her wits.

"I don't know where it is," Summer repeated. She glanced up in time to see Anna's eyes flit to the corner of the woodpile again, then back.

Summer pretended to watch a bird flutter past. The branches were matted together on that side—it was the prunings from two or three years ago and the wood was gray with age.

"Summer!"

Mistress Weller's voice was so shrill that Summer flinched, startled. She heard Letty laugh nervously. Anna stood still as stone, except her eyes, glancing back and forth.

Mistress Weller's face was pink with fury. "Summer, explain yourself or I will advise my husband to get you out of our home at his earliest opportunity. There are places that will have thieves and liars if they are sold cheaply enough, for rough enough work."

Summer bit her lip. There, it had been said aloud at last. And in an angry, threatening manner.

She shook her head, imagining never being able to see James again. Her heart ached. And how could she leave Paris? Or Dody?

A faint melody—one of the field hands singing a slow mournful song—drifted in across the orchard. Summer closed her eyes and listened. The sadness of the tune was almost more than she could bear. Ephrim's hammer had stopped, she realized as the song ended. She looked down the row to see him climbing down his pole ladder.

"Whether or not you are the thief, this sullenness is beyond my tolerance," Mistress Weller said. "Either speak or—"

"Why don't we just look around, Mother?" Letty interrupted. Mistress Weller looked displeased, but she turned, her wide skirt rustling across the carpet of broken twigs.

"Here's a place that's been disturbed," Rob said, staring at the ground. He knelt and poked around, then picked up a stout stick and scratched at the soil. Summer was pretty sure he had chosen the place she had dug.

Everyone watched Rob work for a minute, then two. His stick raked back and forth—but he found nothing. He backed up a little and started over. Summer looked at Anna. She had turned toward Rob, her back squarely toward the corner of the woodpile she had been glancing at.

"Is it out here, Summer?" Mistress Weller demanded. "Are we wasting our time looking?"

Summer shook her head. "I didn't hide anything out here," she said carefully. It would be easy to blurt out that Anna had been the one out here digging, but then she would have to say that Toby had told her. If Anna denied it, then Toby would come under question. Anna's silence puzzled Summer. Had she hidden the ring out here? Why hadn't she mentioned looking for flower arrangement twigs by now?

Summer pressed her lips closed. Anna was staring out into the distance now, up the hill toward the garden. Her face was calm and composed. Summer looked back at Mistress Weller. Taking a quick breath, she tried to speak clearly and loudly. "I didn't steal your ring and I didn't hide anything out here."

Letty had been watching Rob. Now she turned around. "Then why were you looking around? Fisk saw you standing right here, digging with a stick. Who else should we suspect?"

"I don't know who took the ring," Summer said.

Mistress Weller took a step or two toward Rob, leaning to see over the sweep of her skirt. Her corset was laced tighter than usual for company. Summer could tell by the way she moved that it was pinching her. Rob kept up his dirt scratching for another minute or two while they all stood silently. Then he rocked back on his heels.

"Mother, this is ridiculous."

Mistress Weller nodded. "It is." She pulled an embroidered hankie from the bosom of her dress and daubed at her eyes. "I am furious with myself for leaving the ring where someone could take it," she said, sniffling. "I just never thought any of our household capable of such a thing."

Summer could see Letty's smirk disappear as her mother began to cry. Anna came to Mistress Weller's side and maneuvered as close as she could, given the width of their skirts. Letty came closer, too, and they stood together like three lanterns of bright silk on the twig-strewn grass.

Rob got to his feet and scanned the ground again, turning in a slow circle. Then he made a sound of disgust and walked back toward the house. "Where are you going?" his mother called after him.

He turned and looked back at her. "To find Toby. We can ride to court and ask Father to come home early to settle this."

Summer saw Mistress Weller nodding. "Thank you, Rob." Then she turned to face her daughters and Summer. "I want to just go on with our work, like this was any other day. Charles will know what to do when he gets here, and that will be soon enough."

Summer walked slowly behind Anna and Letty as Mistress Weller shooed them all back toward the house. "Letty and Anna, please go change back to everyday gowns. Wearing our best outdoors like this, fraying our hems . . . I don't know what has gotten into me."

"Summer, see to James and then go back out and help Paris as you were told to."

"Mother, I—" Letty began, but her mother cut her off.

"We will rely on your father in this matter, Letty," Mistress Weller interrupted her. "I want to hear no more about it until he comes home."

The sound of hoofbeats made them all look up. Rob and Toby were riding out of the stables at the far end of the slave quarters. Rob gave his mother a gallant wave and then urged his horse into a gallop, rising in the stirrups to lean forward over its neck. Toby's old roan mare cantered valiantly, trying to keep up with the long-legged gelding Rob rode as they raced down the lane. Summer watched them for a few seconds, then turned toward the house before Mistress Weller could say anything more to her.

Paris had changed James's swaddling and had put him to sleep in his cradle. Summer was grateful that he needed no attention just now. She paced, listening to Mistress Weller's voice and the murmurs of Letty and Anna as they drifted down the hallway. Anna had hidden something out at the woodpile, Summer was fairly sure, but what? Anna would not steal her mother's ring. Letty might, Summer heard herself thinking, and pushed it aside. Why would either girl steal something they knew would cause endless trouble? Besides, they had rings of their own.

"I am going to rest," Mistress Weller's voice came again, more distinctly. She was coming closer. Summer crossed to the cradle just as her door opened.

"Is James content?"

Summer turned respectfully. "Yes, Mistress Weller."

Mistress Weller lifted her eyebrows. "Well, then? Run along to help Paris. I'll send Zilpha to fetch you when James wakens and cries."

"Thank you, ma'am," Summer managed, uneasy with the stern coldness in Mistress Weller's voice. *I did not steal your ring*, Summer wanted to shout, but she knew it was no use. Not unless she could prove it—or prove that someone else had.

Summer stood still as Mistress Weller stepped back into the passageway, pointedly leaving the door standing wide open. Paris was wrong this time. Staying clear of the trouble was no longer a possibility. It didn't matter that she was innocent. She had to find the thief, and the ring. And she had to do it before her master got home.

CHAPTER ELEVEN

Summer went down the passageway, meeting Letty's angry eyes, then Anna's thoughtful ones as she passed. Outside, the day was cooling a little, and the plank walk creaked beneath Summer's bare feet.

Paris looked up from the worktable as Summer came into the kitchen. She was cutting the meat from a pig carcass. The ribs jutted up in a short arch. The hams were already cut free and Paris had begun stripping the ribs of flesh for the stewpot.

Summer saw the pickling crock standing by the door. She could smell the sweet and sharp odor of the vinegar and honey. "I'm sorry I didn't help very much," Summer said when Paris didn't speak.

Paris stopped chopping. "I am afraid to ask. Will you just tell me what happened?"

Summer explained quickly, then held up a hand when Paris wanted to ask a question. "I must ask you a favor."

"I see." Paris waited.

"Just tell them you sent me out to the garden for cabbage. If they come."

Paris frowned. "Who?"

"Anyone. Mistress Weller especially, or Letty."

Paris frowned again. "You'll be quick about this, whatever it is?"

Summer nodded. "I swear it."

"Be careful," Paris said, then went back to her chopping, shaking her head, a scowl on her handsome face. Summer watched her for a few seconds, half expecting her to say something else. When she didn't, Summer took down the garden basket and hurried out the door.

She hurried along the back of the great house, her heart already beating like bird wings in her chest. The parlor windows were still tightly curtained and she could hear no voices as she passed. She tried not to glance behind herself more than once as she walked along the house side of the hedge, following the narrow path uphill. She ran through the tall grass above the springhouse, then past it to the edge of the garden.

Stopping, Summer set down the basket and turned, focusing her attention on the row of cabins below. The porches were all empty. So were the rooftops. The pinging of the hammer had indeed stopped—Old Ephrim might be taking a rest. He sometimes sat with Myrna, Summer knew, in the afternoons. They would be the only two around until the field hands were finished for the day—which was two or three hours away. Summer went through the household in her mind, ticking off one name after another.

Zilpha would be helping the girls change their gowns, and probably Mistress Weller as well. That would take an hour, perhaps longer. Toby and Rob were gone, riding to court to fetch Master Weller and Thomas Kyler. Dody and Frieda would be preoccupied with their work, as would Fisk.

Summer looked past the cabins to the south, toward the overseer's house. Sam Eagan was rarely around the great house except late in the evenings, to ask Master Weller about the morrow's work. His wife hated the Negroes for some reason and never came out to the cabins to visit—and she was not invited to the great house very often. Summer knew this was likely the best time she would ever find.

Summer glanced nervously back at the hedge before she gathered her skirts and ran toward the woodpile. Halfway there, she slowed to a walk, realizing how suspicious she looked, tearing across the yard like a dishonest stroller caught out in a cheat of some kind.

I could be a stroller by morning, she thought, scaring herself. As awful as it was to imagine leaving this house to go to another, the idea of being without a family—completely alone in the world, was more frightening yet. Respectable people wouldn't let someone like that into their parlors; visitors to Weller Plantation usually came with a letter of introduction from a family Master Weller knew, or had heard praised by friends.

Summer sprinted. She knew that every step away from the garden made her less likely to be able to defend what she was doing if anyone should come suddenly through the gap in the hedgerow, looking for her. As she approached the woodpile, her breathing was quick and light. This would not take long.

Summer did not hesitate—she didn't waste time poking around aimlessly. She went right to the place where Anna's eyes had strayed. She dropped to her knees and ran her hands through the leaves and twigs, searching for loose soil.

As the seconds ticked past, she began to think she wasn't going to find anything at all. Anna had stared at this corner of the woodpile, she was sure. But maybe she had seen a mouse. Or a spider—or maybe she had just been thinking, staring at nothing.

Summer moved a little to one side, looking up to make sure no one was nearby. A ring was such a tiny thing. She flicked at some dried leaves, then raked them away. Nothing. Then she noticed a pile of twigs that looked odd.

The pile was too perfect, not rain beaten and

wind scattered like the rest of the apple branches that had been thrown here by the field slaves. Trembling, Summer leaned forward and pushed at the too tidy little pile. It slid easily aside, revealing a patch of brown dirt beneath.

Summer began to dig, forcing herself to go slowly, carefully, afraid she might somehow miss the ring, if it was here. An instant later, she sat back and let out her breath in an astonished whoosh. There, peeking from beneath the dirt, was the greenish cover of her sketchbook!

It took Summer only a second to recover from her surprise. She pulled the book free of the soil, then pushed the dirt back into place, repositioning the stack of twigs to conceal it again. Then she stood up, hugging her diary to her chest. There was no one in sight.

Summer walked fast, trying to think. Why would *Anna* have buried her diary? Why would she even have known about it? Letty must have shown her. But why would Anna want to protect me, Summer wondered.

Summer veered uphill toward the garden, away from the silent row of cabins. Halfway up, she heard voices from behind the great house. Heart pounding, she sprinted to the edge of the garden and shoved her sketchbook beneath the broad scalloped leaves of the cabbage that grew farthest from the path. A second later, while Summer was still bent over, Anna came around the end of the house, Letty close behind her.

"There you are!"

Summer pretended to be startled and stood up. "Yes, Mistress Anna?" She tried hard not to sound breathless.

"Mother told us to keep an eye on you!" Letty called, and Anna turned to glare at her.

"I apologize for Letty's terrible manners," Anna said as they got closer.

Summer glanced down. The corner of her diary showed just a little. She nudged at it with her toe, then took a step forward. Anna and Letty had stopped a few paces away on the path. They would not want to step into the loose soil and stain their slippers.

Letty was eyeing the empty basket. "Paris said she sent you out for cabbage."

Summer nodded.

"Well, what's taking you so long?"

Summer shrugged and bent to pull a cabbage from the ground, an enormous head-sized ball that would barely fit into the basket. "I am finished now." She stood still, hoping they would begin the walk back, so that she could follow them. But they waited, as though she was supposed to lead the way. Remembering how Anna's glances had alerted her to the presence of her diary, Summer refused to look back even once.

"My sister absolutely insists you are the one who took my mother's ring," Anna said.

"I am not," Summer told her, turning to look into her eyes. "I would not steal from anyone."

Anna held her gaze for a moment, then looked down, lifting her skirts as she stepped through the deep grass above the springhouse.

Summer led the way back to the great house, fighting tears, resisting a wild urge to demand to know why Letty was convinced of her guilt. But she knew her anger would not be tolerated, nor would passion or shouting. Any behavior of that kind would end in her leaving Weller Plantation almost as surely as Letty's false accusations. Summer tried to calm herself. At least Letty no longer had her sketchbook. Whatever else happened, Master Weller would not read unflattering accounts of himself—nor see her arithmetic or her long essays on logical thinking.

Summer glanced at Letty and Anna, walking beside her. Did they ever long to read the books their brothers read? They were wearing everyday gowns now, and their less expensive wigs. Still, their dresses were finer than anything she would ever wear. Their stays were laced tightly—more tightly than she could ever pull her own—because they would not have to bend or stoop or work. But still, they would not be allowed to read or learn as Rob and Collier would. Did they care?

Summer looked up at the sun. It was in the west now, past meridian. How much longer before Master Weller came home? Summer found herself staring at her own right hand, clenched around the basket handle. Her knuckles were white and the lye scars were an ugly, livid red. "I had better get the cabbage to Paris," she said, giving in to an impulse to flee Letty's and Anna's pretty dresses and their soft pink hands. Barefoot, bareheaded, she began to run.

"Summer!"

It was Letty's voice.

Summer just kept running.

CHAPTER TWELVE

Summer turned into the cookhouse and banged the door closed behind herself.

"Oh, my!" Paris exclaimed, stepping back from the hearth. "Summer? You startled me. Are you—"

"Is James all right?" Summer asked, interrupting.

Paris nodded. "Sound asleep. I went to look a few minutes ago."

Summer hugged her. "Thank you. Thank you so much, Paris."

Paris nodded. She tilted her head. "I hear Missy Anna's voice. Are they right outside?"

Summer looked toward the door. "Perhaps. Letty will not stop accusing me!" she whispered, setting the basket onto the worktable next to the pig carcass.

Paris shook her head. "Master Weller will find the bottom of all this. When he comes home—" Paris began.

"He will believe his daughter," Summer cut her off.

"They came looking for you," Paris told her. "Both of them."

Summer nodded. "I know, they came up to the garden. Mistress Weller sent them to keep an eye on me. I have just run down the hill to get away from them for a few minutes. I have to decide what to do, Paris. I have to be able to think and I—"

Summer's eyes fell on the cabbage and she paused. "May I go wash this for you? If I go up to the well, they won't follow me. The path is always wet below the springhouse."

Paris nodded. "You could go to the storeroom. It's closer, and quiet."

"No. They'll just follow me there," Summer said quickly. She couldn't explain to Paris, but she had to get back up to the garden. Too many people from the cabins went to get vegetables or pull weeds every day.

Paris nodded. "Take the cabbage, then."

Summer hugged her again, quickly, then turned toward the door. When she pulled it open, she was surprised to see Anna standing alone.

"Letty has gone to get something. She says it will show me just how improper and disrespectful you are, how likely to be the thief." Anna's voice sounded weary. "Do you know what she means by that?"

Summer glanced back at Paris, who was pretending to be busy at the hearth. "No," Summer said, trying to keep her voice level. It had to be the sketchbook. So now Letty would discover it was gone.

Anna lifted her shoulders, then let them drop. "Letty seems overwrought," she said carefully.

Summer took one step forward, searching Anna's eyes. Surely she knew that Letty must be talking about the sketchbook, too. Anna, out of all the household, knew the truth about her diary. And she knew that Letty would not find it in its original hiding place.

At that instant, Letty burst from the great house door, her face contorted with anger.

"Where did you put it?" she nearly shouted at Summer.

Summer stepped back to push the cookhouse door closed. Whatever was going to happen, Paris did not need to become entangled.

"You came into our bedchamber, didn't you?" Letty fumed. "Without our permission, you came in. And you took it."

Summer shook her head. "I have not been in your chamber since you invited me in to help you decide on the cloth for your newest dress, three months ago." Summer glanced at Anna, waiting for her to say something, but she didn't.

"That's a lie. You took the sketchbook from my clothespress!" Letty said.

"I did not," Summer said very carefully. She glanced at Anna, who still stood silently, an intent expression on her face.

"Who else would have done it?" Letty went on. "It's just like the ring. Who else in this house would have—"

"I took it," Anna said abruptly. Summer turned.

Letty made a little choking sound and swung

around to face her sister. "Why would you take it?" The anger was draining out of Letty's voice, replaced by astonishment.

Anna shook her head, touching her wig to keep it in place. "I took it to hide it, sure that if Papa saw what you were writing he would—"

"What *I* was writing!" Letty flared. Then she fell silent, fidgeting beneath her sister's piercing stare.

Summer stood very still for a few seconds as the sisters stared at each other. Then she stepped forward. "Paris has asked me to wash this. I had better be about my work. This is none of my concern, is it?"

"Of course it is," Letty objected. "You know which sketchbook I mean."

Summer shook her head. "I recall your father giving me one, but I must have mislaid it. I never had time to draw anyway. I am not a young lady like yourselves. I am just a servant." Then, without allowing Letty another chance to speak, Summer walked away, going as fast as she dared without actually running. Halfway to the springhouse, she glanced back. Letty and Anna were still standing just outside the cookhouse, their heads close together, their hooped skirts touching.

"Missy Summer?"

Summer stumbled, startled, then looked around. It was Dody's voice. "Where are you?"

"Over here. In the grass. Summer, I have to talk to you."

Summer scanned the hillside above the spring-house. There. Dody was crouching, her eyes wide. "Meet me at the well?" Summer asked, keeping her voice low. Dody nodded and scrambled backward, disappearing into the thick grass stems.

Summer glanced back again and almost groaned aloud. Anna and Letty were coming up the path, already too close to pretend she hadn't seen them.

"Summer!" Letty called. "Wait for us."

Her stomach knotting, Summer nodded. She watched Letty and Anna as they picked their way along the path, their skirts lifted.

Letty was leading the way. "Anna thought your sketchbook was mine," she said as she got close. "She hid it so Papa wouldn't get angry at me!" She was smiling. "But I know where it is now. It's out by the woodpile—that's where Anna put it!"

Summer stared at Anna. She had done it to protect her sister? Well, at least that much made sense now. If Anna had known the sketchbook was hers, what would she have done with it? Shown it to Master Weller?

Summer very deliberately looked back toward the great house, away from the garden and the tall grass that had hidden Dody seconds before. Was she still there? Was she listening?

"I was afraid Rob would dig it up," Anna said. "I am so sorry that you were put through the charade of being hauled out there—I can't imagine why anyone who saw me thought it was you. Fisk was mixed up about everything, wasn't he? Even the time."

Summer nodded, looking at Anna's bright swaying dress, then her own frayed apron. No one could have mixed them up, but if Anna wanted to believe it was possible. . . .

"But I am still positive that she is the one who stole Mother's ring, Anna," Letty said, tugging at her sister's sleeve.

Anna pulled free. "Letty, will you please lower your voice. This kind of behavior is what made me think the book was yours. Clutching at my bodice and being shrill! You are not ladylike!"

"Paris needs the cabbage washed," Summer said quietly. She turned once more, denying herself even a quick glance at the garden or at Letty's face, keeping her eyes away from the tall grass.

"We will come with you," Letty was saying, picking up her skirts.

Anna nodded. "I suppose we must."

Summer shrugged and started walking, taking longer strides than usual, leading them uphill past the springhouse, then down again. Where the path got muddy, she speeded up, her bare feet squishing in the wet soil.

"Wait," Letty called out.

"We can't go any farther, Letty," Anna said in a low voice. "Letty, stop. We'll just wait for her here."

Summer turned around. "It's always muddy here. You know that, Letty."

"I never use this path. I never carry water," Letty said indignantly.

"But we used to play up here sometimes, remember?" Summer said quietly. "You and Dody and I." Letty frowned and Summer turned back toward the well, the basket swinging from her hand. She could hear them talking behind her, their exchange quick and argumentative. After a moment or two, Anna called out.

"Summer? We'll be back in a few moments. Don't leave the well until we return. Wait for us." Her voice was officious, stern and cool like her mother's often was.

"Yes, Mistress," Summer called over her shoulder, her heart aching as she went around the final bend in the path. The afternoon sunlight was warm on her shoulders, but she found herself chilly, her arms covered with gooseflesh. She set the basket on the well bench and stood very still.

"Sssst! Summer?" Dody stood up slowly from behind the rocked wall that surrounded the well.

Summer glanced back. Letty and Anna had topped the rise and their bright skirts were disappearing as they started down the other side again.

"I was afraid they were going to come with you. I wasn't sure where I'd run to."

"It's too muddy for their slippers," Summer said evenly, thumping the basket down on the well bench.

"I'm glad they didn't come," Dody said.

Summer sat down heavily beside the basket, feeling the hot sting of tears rising in her eyes. Anna and Letty were, no doubt, on their way to the woodpile now. In a few minutes, they would be badgering at her again, furious that the sketchbook wasn't there. She wanted to run to the garden and get it, but they'd see her now. Summer sighed. Master Weller would come home soon and Letty would convince him that being up in the middle of the night and being locked outside somehow constituted guilt of theft.

Summer shook her head. It made no sense. Letty knew exactly what had happened in the night. She had only found the sketchbook by mistake—and then taken it. *She* was the one who had actually stolen something. Summer sat up straighter and looked at Dody. "Letty is just so certain that I'm the thief and I cannot see how to prove myself innocent."

"I remembered something," Dody said. "I don't know if it means anything or not."

Summer leaned forward. "Remembered what?"

"Remember, on soapmaking day, how Letty and Anna took baths that evening?"

Summer nodded. "I had to bring Letty fresh drawers. And another dry flannel for Anna too, later."

Dody looked thoughtful. "I carried hot water

from the cook hearth in buckets for both of them. Mistress Weller won't let Fisk or Toby anymore, not even for Letty—it's usually me or Frieda or Paris."

Summer watched Dody sit back. "When I brought in the last bucket, Mistress Letty was searching through her clothes, shaking everything out—she hadn't even gotten into the bath yet. She was crying."

Summer nodded slowly. "Did you ask her what was wrong?"

"Of course," Dody said.

Summer waited, glancing up the hill. The path was still empty.

"She said something that made no sense at all to me," Dody went on. "You know how Letty gets. Excited about nothing, angry over less. She kept saying that her mother was going to be furious."

Summer stood up. "Furious about what?"

"I don't know. But she said it was your fault, not hers. I thought it was something with her clothes, a stain or something."

Summer shook her head, trying to make sense of everything, not liking the direction her thoughts were leading her.

Dody shrugged. "I have to tell you something else, Summer. I found something in the cabbage patch," she said slowly.

Summer turned to stare at her.

CHAPTER THIRTEEN

"Where did you put it? Did you . . ." Summer felt the tears start to spill over and Dody jumped up.

"Don't cry, Miss Summer, please. I only wanted to ask you if it was yours. And I wanted to ask you . . . can you write? Is all that writing yours?"

Summer nodded slowly. "Please don't show it to anyone else, Dody, or tell anyone about it. It has caused me nothing but trouble. I wish I had never learned," she added, clenching her hands into fists.

"You don't mean that," Dody scolded her. "I have always wished I could."

"Write?" Summer wiped at her eyes.

Dody nodded. "Read and write. Toby says when we can read and write, there will be no more slavery."

Summer thought about it. "Maybe. Then Negroes could study all the laws and help run the courts and read land contracts like Master Weller does."

Dody was fiddling with the hem of her shift, silent. When she did speak again, her voice was soft and her words were rushed. "Your book is behind the well. I won't tell anybody about it, but will you teach me to read?" She lifted her head and Summer followed her glance. The path was still empty. "Please, Summer?"

Summer nodded. "I think I could. If they don't sell me away. I learned just sitting with Letty and Anna when Mistress Weller taught them the letters."

Dody stood up. "They always made me leave, remember? I usually played on the cookhouse floor out with Paris while I waited." She looked up the hill again. "I don't see them yet."

"They won't be long," Summer said. She went to the far side of the well. There was her sketchbook, leaned primly up against the rocks. Dody had wiped the garden soil from the cover.

What would happen to her if she were caught teaching a slave girl to read? Summer wondered. Paris read a little. She could read receipts that Mistress Weller's lady friends copied out. And Toby could read some, she was pretty sure. Maybe no one would mind.

"But Dody?" Summer said aloud. "It might be best to keep it a secret."

"My whole life is full of secrets," Dody said. "What's one more?"

"Is it?" Summer asked her, picking up the bucket and throwing it into the well. "Your life, I mean. Is it full of secrets?" The bucket hit flat and she tugged the rope to tip it.

Dody came to stand next to her. "The field hands hate us that live up here close to the great house, you know," she said.

Summer shook her head, thinking of the work gangs she saw walking along the borders of the home place, dressed in rags, their heads low. "It isn't hard to imagine why."

Dody nodded. "We eat better, get better clothes. We don't get broken-up backs and knees and sores from the tobacco sacks. We learn to talk different from them." She shrugged. "It was pure luck for me. Mistress Letty picked me for a playmate when I was four. They lined up six or seven of us little girls as I recall. And she pointed at me."

Summer stared at the cotton shift Dody wore— it looked like an oversized man's shirt, and Dody wore nothing beneath it. Then she realized that Dody was staring at her dress. Hoopless and rough as it was, it was certainly better than a shift. And she had under-clothes.

"My father works the tobacco fields," Dody said as Summer hauled the bucket upward. "And my uncles and my brothers. So any little good that comes to me here," she finished up, "I keep secret. I go home at night to the cabins out east of Eagan's house."

"I miss my family so much," Summer said, without meaning to. "They haven't written and I am so afraid for them." She blushed, amazed that she had said it.

Dody nodded, a deep, slow movement. "Master Weller sold my mother two years ago, off to Holt County."

"I'm sorry," Summer said, ashamed that she had not known it. Her voice sounded brittle and the words seemed hollow, useless.

Dody lifted her head but didn't speak for a long moment. When she did, her voice was level, controlled. "I saw them come up after you when you were in the garden . . . Mistress Letty and Mistress Anna, I mean. I saw you come up from the woodpile just before that. That's why I went looking. I thought you might be hiding the ring until I saw your book. I am sorry I thought it."

"I didn't take it," Summer said. "I wish I knew who had."

They were both silent for a few seconds, then Dody's eyes sparkled. "You really will teach me to read and write?" Dody asked, smiling so sweetly that Summer could only nod and put out her hand.

"I have missed our playing. I've missed you."

Dody grasped her hand and squeezed it. Summer pulled in a deep breath and carried the bucket, rope trailing behind, to the well bench. She sluiced water over the cabbage, turning the head upright to wash out the soft green worms that were always under the first layer of loose leaves. "I have to reason this through," Summer said, more to herself than to Dody.

Then she raised her eyes. "That's what Thomas Kyler says. You can reason anything through and find a solution."

"You just be clever, Missy Summer," Dody said. "I don't want you to go anywhere else."

Summer felt tears stinging her eyes again. "I am going to take my book back to the cookhouse, under the cabbage, Dody."

"The water will besmirch the ink," Dody said. "I can keep it for you—"

"No thank you, Dody," Summer stopped her. "I am only going to burn it. So ink smears won't matter."

Dody nodded sorrowfully. "All that writing."

Summer got a second bucket of water and finished the cabbage, shaking out the broad leaves like starched, still wet petticoats over the ground.

"I hear them coming," Dody said as she brought the sketchbook and placed it in the basket. She positioned the cabbage on top of it, loosening the leaves a little so the edges of the cover were completely concealed.

Summer listened. She could hear the sound of high-pitched voices, too. "Letty is arguing or upset."

Dody mimicked surprise. "Maybe she misplaced something."

Summer nodded, thinking hard. Letty was not going to see it that way. She had stolen the sketchbook only to lose it twice now. A sudden thought struck Summer and she stood silently, thinking hard, waiting for Letty and Anna to come.

"What are you pondering so?" Dody asked. "Your face looks like a thunderstorm."

Summer bit at her lip. "I am nearly sure Letty stole the ring."

Dody's eyes widened. "She wouldn't."

"But we all thought Anna might have," Summer protested.

Dody was shaking her head. "Only because Toby saw her digging out there."

"Burying my sketchbook," Summer finished for her. "To save her sister a punishment. Nothing to do with the ring at all."

"Mistress Anna tries to do right. She will make a good wife and mother." Dody sounded so much like Paris or one of the other older women that Summer could only smile at her pronouncement.

The voices were getting closer. Summer found she could understand them.

"I am telling you, that's where I put it," Anna's voice drifted to her ears. They were still out of sight, just on the other side of the hill.

"Why did you have to put it *anywhere?*" Letty demanded as they came into sight. "Why did you have to take it out of the house at all?"

"You know why," Anna argued as they came over the top of the rise and started down. Even her voice was a little shrill now and as Summer watched them walk toward her, she could see their hooped skirts scudding through the weeds. The paths were not nearly wide enough for them to pass.

"There she is," Letty said, pointing at Summer.

"You said she wouldn't be here if she was the one," Anna scoffed. "One of the slaves probably found it. You'll never see it again."

"No one else knew where it was," Letty said.

"Everyone seems to have known there was something in that woodpile," Anna said. Then she noticed Dody. "Hello," she called. "I hope you aren't mixed up in all this, are you?"

Dody shook her head and Anna smiled approvingly as she came to an uncertain stop where the path turned to mud. "I am glad," she said.

Letty didn't speak at all, not even to acknowledge Dody. Summer stared at Letty and Anna as they stood awkwardly in their wide skirts. They looked different to her somehow. The late sunlight bronzed their white wigs, glazed the brocade and silk of their dresses. Letty's wig was slightly askew, Summer noticed. Anna was slapping at a mosquito on her arm, her hoops quivering with the violent motion. The right side of her skirt was tilted oddly, hung up in the grass.

"Are you finished here?" Anna asked.

Summer nodded. She gave Dody a smile and

got one back. Letty was staring off toward the great house, ignoring Dody. Anna waited politely. Summer murmured a good-bye and got one more bright flash of a smile from Dody. Then she started up the hill, gathering her narrow skirt with one hand, carrying the cabbage basket in the other.

Summer stepped off the path to get around Letty and Anna, and led the way back to the top of the rise, thinking hard. She had three things to do before this night was over in order to prove she had not stolen the ring. And she meant to do them all, one by one.

"Where's the sketchbook?" Letty asked as they started down, veering toward the cookhouse.

Anna made a face. "Why do you care? It's hers. It's none of your concern, or Papa's really, so long as she doesn't shirk in her work."

"Where is it?" Letty insisted.

Summer shrugged and smiled. "In your ear? On the moon? Under the tenth plank of the cookhouse walk?"

"What are you talking about?" Anna asked in a terse voice.

"It's a game Letty likes to play. Those were clues," Summer said.

"Then you do have it?" Anna demanded. "At least tell her, so she won't scare the girls that work in the garden to death threatening them to find out where it went."

Letty's face flushed. "I didn't threaten them. I just told them not to lie about finding it—that it had to be returned to me." Letty glanced at Summer. Then she began to walk faster, making her way around Anna as they walked on the path toward the yard.

By the time Summer and Anna came close to the great house, Letty was already kneeling by the plank walk, reaching beneath the board. Anna stopped to ask her what she was doing as Summer walked past them both and went through the cookhouse door, closing it behind herself.

Holding up one hand to silence Paris, Summer swooped her book out of the basket and opened it wide to lay it on the flames of the stew fire. The paper crackled and caught on fire almost instantly.

Summer could hear Anna and Letty arguing as her sketchbook burned into ash, the damp covers arching like a crow's wings.

CHAPTER FOURTEEN

"Dody told me something," Summer whispered to Paris as the book burned and the argument went on outside the door. "She said that Letty was upset on bath night, tossing her clothing around."

Paris waited while Summer paced away from her, then turned back.

"I think she took the ring, Paris. But the only way Master and Mistress Weller are ever going to believe that Letty is responsible for this is to hear her say it herself."

"She never will," Paris said.

"No one knew about the ring being missing back on Friday, did they?" Summer asked.

Paris shook her head. "No. But Mistress Weller doesn't wear that ring often, she said so herself. So she didn't miss it for a few days."

Summer nodded. It was all beginning to make sense. It was *logical*. "Letty didn't mean to steal it," she said aloud. "She just doesn't want to admit that she took it without permission and she can't just put it back because she's lost it."

"So she's blaming you."

"Yes," Summer agreed. "But I don't think she really planned that, either, or she would have thought it out better. She just saw a chance to make me look suspicious to her father and she took it by barring the door. He might think later that I was out hiding the ring."

Paris was nodding, her face thoughtful. "It could be that's how it all happened."

Summer noticed a sudden silence outside the door. She strained to hear, but the girls' voices had stopped completely. Maybe they had gone inside. She turned back to Paris.

"I think I know a way—" A sharp thudding on the door cut Summer off. An instant later it opened and Master Weller came in. His face was dark with fatigue and anger.

"Summer, you must come with me."

Paris made a little sound of dismay and Master Weller shot her a look of warning. "This is not your concern, Paris. Come, Summer."

Summer felt her heart constrict. She nodded stiffly to Paris, then walked ahead of Master Weller, back out the door and across the plank walk. Once they were inside the passageway, he turned, motioning her toward the parlor. "Wait in there." He looked down at her feet, still muddy from the well path, and made a sound of disapproval. "You are not a field slave, Summer. You are expected to keep yourself clean."

Summer kept her eyes down. She was thinking furiously. Then a little trill of crying came down the passageway and shattered her thoughts. "That's James," she said aloud.

Master Weller glared at her. "I am well aware of your duties, Summer. More so than you seem to be. Go in and see to him."

"It will be time to change his swaddling now, Master Weller," Summer said.

"Stay in your room until I come for you, then," Master Weller said. "I have other matters to attend."

Summer nodded again and watched him walk toward the parlor. "Clean your feet, first," he said, turning back just before he went in. Summer could hear Sam Eagan's voice as Master Weller went through the door and closed it behind himself. She whirled and ran out to the cookhouse. "James is crying but Master Weller said I had to wash my feet," she blurted out as she came through the door.

Paris left off her stirring and pointed at a half full bucket of water. "Use that. I'll get Fisk to fetch me another one later."

"Thank him for me," Summer said as she picked up the bucket. She trotted to the edge of the boardwalk and sat down. Bending forward awkwardly, she tipped the bucket to drench her feet. Trembling with fear and hurry, she used a wad of grass to loosen the mud, then poured water over them again, squinting to see any that had clung to her skin. The light was fading, she realized. It was close to sunset. Standing up, she nearly stumbled into Paris and gasped in a startled breath.

"Once you have James swaddled, I could take him out to Myrna for an hour or two."

Summer reached out to touch her cheek. "Thank you. I am supposed to stay in my room—"

"I'll come get him in a little while," Paris said quickly. Then she stood watching as Summer started away. "God bless you," she said quietly just as Summer turned into the dark passageway. Summer clung to the kindness in Paris's voice as she stepped back into the great house.

James was wet through and Summer tried to talk nonsense to him like she usually did to calm him, but it was hard. Working mechanically, she unwrapped his legs, then his arms and torso, then the stay band that held his head still. As always, he kicked hard, flailing his arms once he was freed.

Summer reached for the washbasin and a piece of clean linen. She used the tiny sliver of the bayberry soap to wash him, then patted his skin dry before she began swaddling him again. Her heart was heavy. She had done her first task, burning the sketchbook, but it was beginning to look like she wouldn't manage more than that.

The scent of the soap made Summer flush with anger. Letty couldn't even manage a simple thing like stirring tallow. Summer checked James's straight pins twice before she put a clean little shirt on him, tying the front. She could smell the bayberry soap on the clean linen, too, and she fought another surge of anger at Letty. Anyone else in the household who couldn't stir tallow would have been reprimanded, maybe even punished. But Letty could play and dawdle because she was Master Weller's daughter and...

An idea formed in her mind and Summer caught her breath as she examined it more closely. It made sense. It was a *logical* explanation for everything.

Knowing that she would be punished if Master Weller came out and found her not in her room, Summer carried James swiftly down the hall, outside, and ran up the plank walk. Once inside the cookhouse, she thrust James at Paris.

"I have to go out to the storeroom," she said breathless. "I can't explain now." She took a candle from the wall sconce and lit it at the fire.

Paris looked startled and nervous, but she nodded as Summer spun around and hurried back out, shielding the candle flame with her hand so she could go fast. She followed the walk halfway to the washhouse, then jumped down and took the well-worn path around the back of the cookhouse. The door was heavily barred against animals and Summer had to set her candle down to open it. The flame flickered, but held, as she dragged the door open wide.

The storeroom was full and orderly, as always. Paris kept it that way. Summer followed the stairs down into the root cellar. Usually, she liked coming out here. She liked the smell of the apple barrels and the sweet odor of the puncheons of cider. Along the back wall, shelves held hogsheads of oil and the casks of Master Weller's peach brandy stood nearby. The soap was down here, too, where the heat of midday couldn't soften it too much. Summer set the candle in a niche in the dirt wall and began searching.

There were fifteen or twenty big blocks of soap, but Summer was only interested in the smaller cakes, the ones that had come from the last batch of tallow and bayberry. The molds were hard to remove without a hot knife, but Summer managed, straining. Then she held each cake up to the candle, her eyes scanning the pebbly surface frantically.

She was on the fifth cake when she heard Master Weller's voice. Blinking back tears of desperation, she kept looking. The sixth and seventh cakes revealed nothing. But the eighth one held an added glimmer in the candlelight, just the tiniest visible fleck of silver. Summer nearly cried out in relief. She tucked the soap into her bodice and blew out the candle. Two done, she thought. Now the hardest of all.

CHAPTER FIFTEEN

Summer tiptoed out of the storeroom. She could hear every voice in the household calling her name in one direction or another, but there was only one she was interested in. Letty's cries were coming from inside the great house.

Summer pushed on the door and slipped inside. It sounded like her master was out in front. Toby was in back. Summer could hear him shouting Dody's name—probably to ask if anyone had seen her.

Summer followed Letty's voice, ducking into the linen storeroom to let Anna pass, then cautiously peeking before she came out and went quietly through the parlor door.

Letty was standing in the open front door, leaning out as far as she could without stepping off the carpet. The day was waning fast, Summer realized. It would be time to light the candles, soon.

"Excuse me, Mistress Letty," she said, as loudly as she could.

Letty jumped, then turned so fast that her skirts caught on the door frame. She struggled to free them, staring at Summer. "Papa!" she screamed. "Papa, she's in here!"

At the sound of her shrieks, Summer crossed the carpet in three or four quick strides and put her hand over Letty's mouth for an instant, startling her into silence. "I will tell your father everything if you don't. Everything. I could have been *sold* over this. Wasn't I ever your friend? Wasn't Dody? How can you not remember?"

She stepped back as people began to pour into the room. Rob was first and he stood at the door like a guard, his arms out as if she would try to dodge past him. Letty's face was angry, then frightened as Toby and her father came in, with Thomas Kyler close behind them. Mistress Weller and Anna came last, hampered by their skirts.

"Summer, I told you to stay in your room," Master Weller said coldly. "This kind of disobedience only makes matters worse."

"I had to go out to the storeroom just for a moment, Master Weller," Summer managed, her voice calmer than she expected it to be. She could feel her heartbeat in her throat and wrists. A sheen of sweat rising on her forehead made her feel clammy and strange.

"To steal something else?" Letty accused.

Her father shook his head. "Enough, Letty." Then he faced Summer. "Where is my wife's ring?"

Summer forced herself to meet his eyes. "I found it. But Letty will have to tell you where."

Letty had turned to stare. "Of course she has it," she said, then paused and looked at her father. "She stole it."

Thomas Kyler was watching Summer intently and she saw him smile just a little. Rob looked interested, not upset. Mistress Weller's face was like stone. "If you have my ring, Summer, I expect you to return it at once."

"Letty?" Summer looked at her.

"You heard my mother," Letty shot back, her eyes darting from her mother to her father, then back.

"Last night, I was barred out of the house," Summer began, then paused, giving Letty a chance to speak. When she did not, Summer stopped and began again. "We made soap on Friday last—"

"I know when we made soap," Letty cut her off. "We all know. What's the point of this?"

"That's the night the ring was borrowed."

"You were never given permission to borrow anything from my bedchamber," Mistress Weller said coldly.

Summer nodded. "Nor did I borrow anything. Someone else did."

Summer saw Toby shuffle uncomfortably and

then go rigid when he realized she was watching him. She longed to signal him that he was not her target, but she couldn't risk losing the suspense she had created. Instead, she swept her eyes across everyone in the room. "It was not intended to be a theft," Summer said very clearly. "No one ever meant to steal anything." She looked at Letty pointedly, wishing she could add, *except my sketchbook.*

Abruptly, Letty leaned close to her ear. "I will tell them about what you wrote."

"Go ahead," Summer whispered back. "But I burned it in the hearth fire, so there will be little to show."

"What's this about," Master Weller demanded. "Letty? Do you know something about this?"

Letty shook her head, but he was staring at her now, not Summer, studying her face as she fidgeted.

"So Friday last, bath night, was the start of the trouble," Thomas Kyler said, prompting Summer to go on.

She nodded. "The borrower came into the cookhouse and fiddled with your ring, Mistress. Putting it on, taking it off."

Mistress Weller was looking less angry and more puzzled.

"And the borrower stayed to help stir the tallow," Summer went on. "Not very well, I might add. The tallow was left unstirred long enough almost to ruin the bayberry batch."

"Which would have meant starting over," came Paris's rich voice from the doorway. "But Summer got back from caring for James and noticed and saved it." Everyone turned and Summer gave Paris a look of gratitude.

"Later, when the borrower got ready for her bath . . ." Summer went on, "She realized the ring was missing." Mistress Weller was staring at Letty now, too. They all were.

"It was right after you came in," Letty exploded at Summer. "You were there, and then you left, and I couldn't find the ring. You took it. You did steal it, even if I was the one to take it out of my mother's bed-chamber."

In the wake of Letty's outburst, there was a thick silence in the room. Master Weller stood up. "Letty? Did you bar Summer from the house last evening?"

Letty nodded, her eyes filling with tears. "But she was up late, writing in that sketchbook of hers and she—"

"Hardly an offense worthy of being barred from the house," Thomas Kyler put in.

Summer pulled the cake of soap from her bodice and handed it to Mistress Weller. "The ring fell into the tallow when Letty was stirring. You can just see it . . ." She pointed to the curving sliver of silver. A murmur of astonishment ran through the room. The soap was passed from hand to hand. Thomas Kyler was smiling.

Anna came to Summer first, her eyes troubled. "I apologize for everything that has happened. All of it," she said, her eyes full of meaning.

"I admire your logical thinking," Thomas Kyler said from behind Anna. Summer flushed.

"I do not approve of any of what you have done, Letty," Master Weller said sternly, passing the soap back to his wife. "But do you see how covering one mistake led to the next? If you had just admitted losing the ring—"

"I know, Father, I know," Letty said, and then she began to cry. Her shoulders shook and Summer watched as Master Weller walked her slowly out of the parlor. Anna followed them.

"Carry on with your regular tasks, everyone," Mistress Weller said formally, then followed the rest, carrying the soap cake in one hand and tilting her hoops to one side with the other so that she could get through the door.

Toby shook his head and winked, then followed Rob and Thomas Kyler out of the room. Only Paris was left. Summer ran to her and was enfolded in a long hug. When she stood back, Paris smiled. "Your mother would have been very proud of you today, Summer. I am."

Only then did Summer begin to cry.

I am writing in a sketchbook that appeared upon my cot this night. A gift from Thomas Kyler, I think. It is the same sort that he gives to Letty and Anna. I have told Master Weller about the book I burned. I was frightened, but I knew that Letty would have told him and I didn't want him to think me dishonest. He says I may write a little, so long as my areas of interest remain proper and I abandon writing out arithmetic and logic. I will refrain from writing them down, certainly.

Master Weller had Letty come to apologize to me. She cried a long time and we parted friends, though not the sort of friends that Paris and Dody have become to me. She truly looked sorry, I must admit. Paris says that Letty will grow out of her faults. Perhaps.

Thomas Kyler came to the cookhouse today while I was helping Paris. He brought me two books he said were suitable for a young lady. I might confide in him about Dody someday. I like him very much.

James is stirring a little. I am tired this night. I have made a decision I wish to record. When I am freed, I am going to try to save up money until I can buy Dody's freedom, and Paris's. We could all live together in one house. How lovely that would be. It's a difficult dream and I know it, but still . . . perhaps there is some reasonable, logical way to achieve it.

James is starting to cry. I will write more tomorrow.

SURVIVAL

Would you get out alive?

FACED WITH NATURAL DISASTER, ORDINARY PEOPLE FIND UNTAPPED DEPTHS OF COURAGE AND DETERMINATION THEY NEVER DREAMED THEY POSSESSED.

Find Adventure in these books!

#1 TITANIC

On a clear April night hundreds of passengers on the *Titanic* find themselves at the mercy of a cold sea. Few will live to remember the disaster—will Gavin and Karolina be among the survivors?

#2 EARTHQUAKE

Can two strangers from very different worlds work together to survive the terror of the quake—crumbling buildings, fire, looting, and chaos?

#3 BLIZZARD

Can a Rocky Mountain rancher's daughter and her rich, spoiled cousin stop arguing long enough to cooperate to survive a sudden, vicious blizzard?

#4 FIRE

Fate and fire throw Nate and Julie together on the dark streets of Chicago. Now they must find a way out before the flames spreading across the city cut off their only chance of escape!